Sherlock Holmes

and the Council of Seven

John Paul Medhurst

SHERLOCK HOLMES AND THE COUNCIL OF SEVEN

ISBN: 979-8-88653-470-2

Melange Books, LLC
White Bear Lake, MN 55110
www.melange-books.com

Published in the United States of America.

Cover Design by Ashley Redbird Designs

For Mum and my great friend Eric

CHAPTER ONE

FOLIE A TROIS

I miss Doctor Watson. I do. I miss him terribly. Silly sod. I would never have told him to his face, of course, I would never have told anybody that. As a rule, when it comes to people, I still prefer their space to their company. I view them in much the same way as I see the English weather. I don't mind the rain, the cold or the wind, I can tolerate them, but not all at the same time. I hate rudeness, laziness and selfishness and I find most lazy people are selfish and most selfish people are rude and more of them are turning out to be all three; the next generation of Brits will be born with fog lamps and flippers, and I can't deal with society anymore.

So, I have retired. I haven't retired from life as such, just from confusion. I have discovered that the human body, much like the planet we populate, is designed to keep going, to replenish and repair itself and that only through the constant onslaught we put our bodies under, are our lifespans considerably shortened.

The reader will become aware that I am undergoing an etheric, alchemical process, a crystallization of the elements in me, a purification and regeneration of my mind and body and for this I need to gather materials from pure sources only.

I have given up the more unreasonable of my vices, though I still like to mingle with the upper reaches of the lowerarchy and general beggary from time to time, but spiritual nutrition can only be found away from the scream of London and in order to complete the transmutation of my cells, they need peace. So, I brought them here to Cornwall, at once my sanctum and my oubliette, and as I take breakfast at the bottom of the garden and gaze out over the bay, I am reminded of the uncommon minds who also came to these shores to convalesce. Charles Dickens, Victor Hugo, Agatha Christie, John Le Carre and Daphne du Maurier all chose to recharge their batteries on the coast. They also came here to write.

Now I'm no scribe, but Dr. Watson has left me with little choice, and it would be a travesty if the events of our last case (the details of which, just like the streets of London, are carved into my very marrow) were left to disintegrate in a filing cabinet in Marylebone, such was the jeweled multiplicity of it. I have often wondered if I could write and which writer I would be like. I imagine my scribblings to be a blend of Bukowski and Dickens; bitey, pragmatic prose with a touch of Victorian swazz, and if Dr. Watson was here now, I would throw my arms around him, I would hold him by the shoulders, look him straight in the eye, and I would tell him from the bottom of my heart, that I loved him and I missed him. And I would, I really would. If I knew where he was.

CHAPTER TWO

MOCK THE WEAK

It was perfectly understandable for Dr. Watson to feel aggrieved, when I mentioned to him that the Greek philosopher, Plutarch, had once stated, that somebody who lived with a lame man, would eventually start to limp. Though we no longer reside under the same roof and the quote is not at all to be taken literally, I did gain some traction in the discussion with the fact that there was A) No smoke without fire and B) With every example in the universe at his disposal, that he should indeed choose that one and for my sake, if not for his own, that if he wasn't going to seek medical advice, then he should at least take up a hobby that would aid in the rehabilitation of his injured leg. Having never seen any physical evidence of said injury, nor any medical papers to support the claim, and given the dictum that all embarrassment turns to anger, I gave up trying and casually assumed that the case was wholly psychosomatic and that Dr. Watson had actually dreamed his limp into existence.

The hobby I had in mind was something slow and sedate, like walking football or ballroom dancing, so my mind was suitably blown when he arrived at my flat one morning with the disturbing news that he had signed up with a local club to go rock climbing. Initially I was horrified by this revelation, so much so that I followed him to Wales, convinced as I now was that Dr. Watson had called my bluff and had every intention of climbing up a mountain with only one working leg. It was, however, to my utter joy and relief that, as I watched from behind a rock, the instructor climbed one meter up the cliff face and then struck out left, marking the hand and footholds in yellow chalk, all at the same height, right to the end for the students to follow.

I snuck home without being spotted and was ready to be impressed after dinner, when Dr. Watson regaled me with heroic tales of how he was nearly blown to his death from the highest peak in Snowdonia. I wondered how close his story of being a mountaineer was to the stories he told of being a soldier, but I guessed the subject was too sensitive to broach and said nothing. I did, however, mention to him that for beginners to take such risks was at the very least negligent and that I would be getting in touch with the club secretary to make my feelings known. This prompted the doctor into a blustery admission, that maybe he had embellished the story somewhat and that he wasn't really that far from the ground at all. Like the friend I am, I had noticed his discomfort and provided him with an escape route, which he gleefully took. I congratulated him on his new hobby and remarked that with plenty of practice and dedication, maybe he could be the first person in history to walk round Everest.

As if to highlight his remarkable progress after just one lesson, the signature knock and scrape of Dr. Watson's feet on my staircase this morning, was a touch lighter and a touch faster than usual. It unnerved me slightly, as I had been up all night sleeping and wasn't ready for him. I looked like I had been pulled backwards out of a pipe and my eyeballs felt like they had been dipped in vinegar. I tried to look as fresh-faced and rested as was possible when the doctor burst through the door all mister-Monday morning. He stood, laptop bag on his shoulder, a raft of newspapers under one arm and his coffee in the other hand. His face fell in disappointment, as he took in the sight of my crumpled frame, still in my dressing gown with a crossbow resting on my lap. It was no use hiding anything from him, he knew me better than Mycroft knew me, hell he knew me better than my parents did. I felt like I'd let him down, but I wasn't about to show it. The doctor set his laptop down, sat himself at the table and opened up the first of the broadsheets he had brought with him. He slurped his coffee and squinted over at me.

"You don't look yourself this morning, Holmes," he said.

"So why are you telling me?"

He breathed a heavy sigh, shook his paper and went back to reading and slurping. There were four or five topics of conversation I wanted to avoid at all costs this morning, but one glance at Dr. Watson and I knew that they were the only topics on his mind and he was just biding his time. I felt trapped in my own flat, maybe we should start meeting elsewhere. Maybe he should work from his own apartment. Maybe I was overthinking it and he wasn't sitting there wondering which sensitive subject he could hit me with first whilst pretending to take in the day's events. He breathed in, as if to say something, didn't and just exhaled. It would come with the next breath for sure. He turned the page, shook the sheets and cleared his throat.

"Middle of a pandemic...Boris Johnson has got his girlfriend pregnant and now he's gone on holiday." "What's the point?"

"Of getting his girlfriend pregnant?"

"Of either. No point in him going on holiday since it'll take two weeks for him to go white. I mean look at him. He looks like he needs a blood transfusion.

"And the pregnancy?"

"You know, Watson, it blows my mind that they allow just anyone to have kids. He's quite clearly a product of weak sperm and now he's allowed to run riot with his watery offering, diluting the gene pool and causing the human race quite irreparable damage. The bumbling toff routine was cute for five minutes. I am afraid, my friend, that the age of the leader is over. We are encouraging the breeding of weak people. We are in the third and final stage of empire, a hedonistic smash and grab, where the rich have created an alternative universe for us to play in while they steal what's left of the other. There is no distance between the left and right anymore. Anybody a smidgen to the right of Stalin is Hitler...blows my bloody head off."

Watson stared at me, but let me finish before he added,

"When are you going to...?"

"I'm not going to have a fucking jab," I shouted. I jumped out of my chair, hung the crossbow back on the wall and started to get changed.

Dr. Watson stared at me in total surprise. He shook his damn paper again.

"Bit jumpy this morning, Holmes," he said. "I wasn't going to ask you about that. You don't have to go anywhere for your jab. I have ordered it from Harley Street, so I'll give you your vaccine. What I was going to ask you is when you are going to meet Grace."

I chastised myself for biting his head off, took a deep breath and started to make some tea.

In return for brow-beating Watson into taking up a hobby, I had foolishly agreed to get some help myself in the form of a lifestyle guru. Now in a strong field, there are two professions I trust less than all others, those being politicians and faith healers and I'd been hit with both subjects at the same time. The former I deal with on an almost daily basis and though I must play the game, I find that they have neither the life or work experience, nor the intelligence to make one single decision on my behalf. Of course, they promise the earth in their initial manifesto, but the second they set up in London with their expense account, their late bar and their flat in Dolphin Square, everything changes. As nowhere in the country is more than two hours from London, ideally all politicians should spend their first year in office, from the place they represent. Governments should be made up of scientists, engineers, doctors, farmers, bakers, nurses and such, not these simpering, over-protected and under-developed public schoolboys.

Case in point, is this bloody pandemic. Now I find, that when something like this is announced, one would be much closer to the truth if you looked immediately in the opposite direction....so that's what I did. When Covid broke, I made a quick scan of what else was going on in the world. Lo and behold we had the annual military games, being held this year in Wuhan, China. I looked at the medal table expecting the USA to sweep the board. they had won a few, but only a fraction of China's haul. What about the United Kingdom? Zero. Wait, what? Look again. UK, zero. Guess why. Because we didn't attend.

A new commercial passenger route had opened from Wuhan to Milan, as China was providing the cheap labor to Italy's fashion industry. So that was where and how, but who? My research led me to a pharmaceutical company in New Jersey, that at one time was the supplier of three out of every five products on a chemist's shelves. Right now, however, they are involved in the manufacturing of one thing and one thing only, male fertility drugs. Alarm bells ringing yet? They might start with the knowledge that this company hailed from a small town in California called Corona. This took me about half an hour to unravel and by teatime I was getting my knuckles rapped by my big brother.

Faith healers, along with shamans, spirit guides and the laughable goddesses are barking up the right tree and do mean well, but there is something important missing from their repertoire I feel.

About twenty years ago, I found that I could do a neat little trick with what I thought to be my diaphragm. At will, I found I was able to create a feeling in my stomach, that was akin to going over a bridge in a car. I could hold this feeling as a long pulse and when I let it go, a powerful surge would course through me. It was a feeling that emanated from the base of my spine and would run down my arms and legs, up my chest and neck and out of my throat. It was a beautiful feeling that made me feel focused, relaxed, very warm and so full of love and I had taken enough good MDMA back in the nineties to recognize it as the exact same feeling. Worried that I was borrowing against future serotonin and creating an imbalance in body that would make me miserable for years to come, I wrote to a couple of neuroscientists for their take on the matter.

They advised me that I was probably bypassing my vagus nerve and gaining access to pleasure cells, but not to worry, as my body would strike its own balance. Wanting to know more, I contacted a few eminent yogis who told me that I was moving Prana, or life-force energy around my body at will, that I was indeed in possession of a great gift and I should treat it with great reverence and care. I learned much later that within this phenomenon, lay the ancient secret of the human body's ability to repair itself, which in turn makes me wonder what is happening with all the energy work that these healers have for sale? And if they aren't talking about this surge, this pulse and this exact feeling, what exactly are they talking about?

CHAPTER THREE

AMAZING GRACE?

I admit that there are some areas of my life in which I do need help. The more unreasonable of my habits were relinquished without much fanfare. The Class As have gone, along with the lifestyle that goes with them, no heroin, no needles, no crack and nothing up my nose. Tobacco has gone too, though I have started to explore the delights of marijuana, taken in the form of my new Vape, an elegant contraption engineered by an Italian friend in Angel. My capacity for aggression has been somewhat reduced, largely due to the horrible revelation that being punched in the face hurts far more than I thought it did. I had no idea that fighting was so painful. Rendered senseless by an assortment of opiates, fights were great fun and were treated much like a game of chess. Not anymore.

My alcohol consumption was also addressed in this shakeup, though the snob in me took longer to let red wine go than I thought it would and was as distressing to give up as the tobacco and when I get to it the coffee, which though I still drink, I drag back out of my body by taking magnesium. Eating fresh tamarind carries the excess fluoride in my body away and I filter all water without exception.

Mrs. Hudson was quite sad when she learned that she would longer be required to provide a roast dinner every Sunday, as I have given up eating things with four legs. This is more in response to my not being able to vouch for the provenance, feed, transport, and treatment of these creatures, so I am down to chicken and fish, which I love anyway and can catch myself should the need arise. All these little things have been given up without ceremony. If I ever feel myself falling, again I call on the masters and between Seneca, Marcus Aurelius and myself, I'm quite confident we can get me on the straight and narrow. To date I have fallen once, though it was under extreme circumstances.

A year ago, Irene Adler, my only love, passed away and though I tried to remain stoic, eventually the strings were cut and my pendulum just swung. For this smaller stuff though, I find no reason to be congratulated and applauded for any of it, like some misguided explorer. I have simply given up things that I shouldn't have been doing in the first place and by doing so, have really only become the hero in a crisis of my own making, a bit like Shackleton.

So, when I reluctantly agreed to take on a lifestyle guru, my acceptance came with a strict caveat, that she (and it must be a girl) must not, under any circumstances, be attractive to me. There's a saying among the hospitality sector in Spain, that warns against sexual relations in the workplace... "Non pongas la polla, donde comes la olla," which loosely translates as "Don't stir your own soup with your dick." We have the same phrase in English. "Don't screw the crew." An extreme example of this philosophy would be a friend of mine, who runs a porn empire in Denmark and steadfastly refuses to hire anybody remotely attractive, as a person with an armful of dildos and butt plugs is less likely to approach the counter if there is somebody attractive stood behind it.

Having seen this philosophy in action, I adopted it without further ado.

Happily, Grace had ruled herself out as potential girlfriend material before I had even set eyes on the girl. I had had two exchanges with her, one phone call and one text, in which she had sent me a suggested meal plan and a fitness calendar that hilariously included yoga.

During our phone call, and with great trepidation, I had asked her at which point in her life she had discovered that she had the ability to heal people. Her answer contained only five words but were the five words that ground my gears like no others. To make matters worse, she delivered them in that crackly, affected, can't-be-arsed, SoCal, valley girl drawl.

She said, "So I like totally manifested."

I stared at my phone in utter disbelief, thinking for all the world that she had been sent by Mycroft. I hung up the call immediately. Let me explain.

The word "So" isn't offensive in the slightest, unless used as the first word at the start of an answer. This started a few years back with scientists, who were being interviewed on the news. The word "I" at the start of any sentence screams "me me me" and should be used much less. Here though it isn't the first word, though having rendered the word "so" redundant already, becomes so and there it stands. "Like" again is a very good word and important when comparing things or expressing one's fondness for something. Under no circumstance is it to be used to approximate a time to meet. "What time shall we book the table for?"

"Like six."

"Seven? Five? Six isn't like six. Six is fucking six."

The word "totally" is self-explanatory and goes together with its nauseating twin, "literally." And we arrive at the most over-used and least understood of all words that have ever existed.... "Manifested!"

Maybe I had gone too far with my expectations of her. I had also admonished myself for not thinking for even one second that she might not even be attracted to me. It made me laugh. Why the hell would she be even remotely interested in me? a skinny middle-aged man with various drug habits, no cooking skills, who doesn't drive, do housework or want children...who sleeps where he falls, wears his heart on his face and goes missing for days on end. What girl in her right mind would want me? Moreover, the case for the prosecution would contest that my greatest deficiency was exactly that, something I didn't do, something I was missing, something that a relationship needed to survive as opposed to any of the numerous objectionable habits I exhibited and that was the fact that any potential partner of mine would never receive the attention she needed from me. Yet here I was outside South Kensington tube station a few hours later, scrubbed and scraped and ready to listen. I was also soaking wet and starving to death...and she was late.

My patience had all but evaporated and I was about to leave when she lit up the sky in front of me. I secretly breathed in as she looked up at me, gathering as much information as I could from the breeze she came in on. She smelled of grass and wardrobes and Dr Bronner soap. Her hair hung in dreadlocks maybe seven years in and framed a flawless, olive-skinned small round face. She had coffee bean eyes of hazel and jade that glittered in the rain. She wore no makeup and looked like she never did. She wore work boots, khaki-colored Carhartt dungarees and a purple faux-fur coat, adorned with badges that meant nothing to me. Her dental work was exquisite, and her nails were short but well-manicured. When she reached her hand out to me, I caught the faint scent of her body, which was musky, sweet and unshaved. At the very least she was a Bonafide hippy. I got the feeling that she didn't need to work, but that she did anyway. She presented and held herself well and had easy, confident control of the space she occupied. So much so that I became aware of myself and hoped that my surprise wasn't detectable to her. She beamed up at me and said in a perfectly clipped home counties accent, "Sherlock Holmes...Grace. I'm sorry I'm three minutes late. Some friends of mine were throwing a surprise treat for my birthday."

I was thunderstruck. "Err...and how was it?" I stammered.

Her smile was captivating. "I have no idea...we rescheduled. I was meeting you." My brain was starting to unravel. I tried to hold myself together. "Your accent. I thought you were from California."

"I'm from Aylesbury."

If her intention had been to throw me off and keep me guessing, then she had succeeded in absolute spades. My heart set a trap for my mouth, and I was careful not to open it too quickly. "And the phone call? All those words you said to me."

"Ah yes, sorry about that. That's why you hung up on me."

I went to speak, but nothing came out. She noticed my discomfort and took her cue.

"So, you're the legendary Sherlock Holmes."

I felt barely adequate. "Err, yes," I replied.

She looked me up and down, still smiling. "I thought you'd be more...." she said.

I gazed back at her, puzzled. "More what?"

Her eyes flashed up at me again, green this time and full of mischief. "I'd finished," she said.

She turned on her heel and marched off. I grabbed hold of a post, as my knees threatened to give way and stared disbelievingly after her through the rain. With some effort, I pulled myself together, straightened my hat, wiped my face and took a deep breath and with my heart doing somersaults, I started to follow her, all the while telling Seneca and Marcus Aurelius to mind their own sodding business. I caught her up and she took my arm, which I tried valiantly to unflex. We set off to find sushi and though it is far away my favorite food in the world to eat, all I could think about right then was soup.

Some twenty minutes later, we were being refused entry to our third restaurant, owing to the water being turned off in the immediate area and the very excellent reason of us having no reservation anywhere. Though she didn't show it, I could feel Grace's mood beginning to slip. I suppose everything is relative to how you want to perceive it though. Maybe it was because she had faithfully trusted her birthday evening to me and the fact that I hadn't bloody booked anywhere, was the reason that I was feeling the weight of expectation getting the upper hand.

The rain had stopped and had left the city in a dense cloud, through which struggled the sound of police sirens, their plaintive wails deadened until the last second, when they burst through the fog beside us and raced by. Cities will be cities, but tonight there was a feeling of panic in the air; something was wrong. No doubt I would get to know exactly what soon enough, but for now my only concern was not to look a fool in front of Grace. We had to get away from here. I had a plan. I didn't like it one bit, but it would work a treat. I stopped, turned to her and held her gently by the shoulders. She smiled, but there was a tear in her eye. She took my hands from her shoulders and squeezed them.

"It's okay, Sherlock. Don't worry about it. Maybe we should have booked. People are just glad to be out again, so everywhere is busy, even on a Monday, let's just leave it." She laughed at herself and wiped her eyes. "Come on, my eyes are getting puffy." I felt horrible. I reached out and wiped a tear away with the back of my finger, confidence and optimism seeping back into me.

"Come on," I said. "Please don't do that. I have an idea. I

didn't want to, but I would never forgive myself if I spoiled your birthday."

My research into the separation of ego and self took over here and I beamed at her, as my proposed plan unfolded in my head without a hitch. I cupped the side of her face with one hand; this was my moment to say something deep and devastating that would fire her brain and melt her heart. I started off badly.

"And I love your chubby face..." I heard myself say..."it suits you." Swerving wildly, I added, "You should cry more often."

Whether Grace spotted my faux pas or actually believed it was a joke matters not; she smiled as she had smiled before, took my arm with redoubled enthusiasm and as we strode off, she snuggled into my shoulder. I thought of our fibers fusing together where we touched. I thought of the transfer of energy between us and wondered what she was feeling right now. While considering this I stopped for a brief second and pretended to get my bearings. What I was really doing was steadying my breath and my legs so that I could send a pulse out to her. I concentrated on the points we were touching and felt the surge go through my chest, through both arms that were entwined with hers, up my spine and the back of my neck, which her cold nose still nuzzled. Whether she felt the energy or not I had no idea, but as we crossed the street, she held on to me like we had known each other for years. We skirted the side of Hyde Park and turned into Belgravia.

"So, where to then?" she asked.

"Oh, not far at all," I said. "And at the same time not far enough. My brother has a private member's club around the corner. The lockdown has finally forced him to embrace the century he is living in and to structure his business accordingly. For the first time in its history, the Diogenes Club is accepting female members, and to claw back some of the revenue they pretend they lost in the pandemic, they have had to diversify. So now they are serving food. Tonight is the soft opening or some such thing and to mark the occasion, I believe they are having a sushi night."

I took my phone from my trouser pocket and sent a quick text. The difference in Grace was profound, the news that all was finally, eventually going to be okay took all the tension from her body in one hit. Her smile was back and her eyes sparkled once more. She laughed. "So why didn't we come here in the first place?" she said. "If you don't like sushi, you should have said something, silly. We could go somewhere else."

"Oh, I adore sushi," I replied.

We rounded the corner and came to a stop in front of an elegant, Regency building that was the Diogenes Club. Mycroft appeared on the top step, hands in his pockets and looked down at us, a smug grin on his face. "It's him I'm not too fond of. Evening Mycroft."

It didn't matter at all to my brother, that Grace and I had appeared at his opening night under desperate circumstances, and that his establishment should be blessed with our presence at all pleased him enormously. I dreaded him finding out it was Grace's birthday to boot. He smirked at me, as we climbed the steps. He addressed me and bowed his head briefly to Grace.

"Well, well, well. Good evening, brothermine. Mademoiselle."

He sidled up to me as we made our way through the grand entrance and spoke out of the side of his mouth.

"I won't embarrass you about masks and jabs in front of your girlfriend, Sherlock."

"Lifestyle coach," I corrected him. "Watson's idea."

Mycroft guided us through the door and signaled an assistant.

"About time. I'm afraid, however, that I'm going to have to disappoint you both. We have had to close the kitchen, and the water has been turned off. Apparently, something or someone has popped up in a drainage channel, and the police are closing off the area as we speak. We could rustle up a few dragon rolls and some edamame for you, but that's about it.

Grace was beaming. I was forgetting myself.

"Grace," I said, "may I introduce my elder and wiser, though far less better-looking brother, Mycroft. Mycroft, Grace; the poor soul who has been hired to steer my reckless soul through retirement...should I ever get to it.

We had entered the grand main hall of the club, a throwback to more regal times. As always it was full of stuffy bloated old businessmen sprawled on oversized leather seats, reading broadsheets and smoking cigars. Plates of sushi were scattered about but largely remained untouched. As usual it was deathly quiet.

An open kitchen had been erected at the back of the room, from where the chefs worked in complete silence. I watched as one chef dispatched a fish "Ikejimi" style, by inserting a thin metal rod vigorously into the back of it, immediately crashing its central nervous system, which he then dropped into an ice-water bath.

I watched transfixed as a ribbon of blood streamed from it as it sank. Something felt strange about the place, but I couldn't put my finger on it. Our coats were taken by our host, Lyra, a striking specimen with a shock of blue hair, dark makeup and a leather trouser suit. She was an impressive female and even though she quite clearly was a man, that's not what was wrong in the club. Then it came to me. I turned to Mycroft.

"I thought tonight was your opening night," I said.

Mycroft smiled at me. "Indeed, it is."

"So where are all the people?"

He looked around, the place was full. "They're here," he said.

I feigned amusement, but a giddy feeling rose in me. "The North Pole has no fixed position," I said, "It constantly moves around and by doing so is really an abstraction, because when you go there, there's actually no "there" to go to. I turned to Grace briefly. "See what I have to put up with? Here, where? I thought there would be more women here," I looked around again. "Well, more than none."

Something flashed in my head and though it was supremely childish, it was funny. I had wanted to do this for a while and had just never remembered, but I couldn't help myself. I borrowed a felt-tip pen from the waiter station and nipped outside. The D very easily became a B and with one stroke of the sharpie, I had changed the elegant sign of my brother's club from the Diogenes to the Biogenes. Giggling to myself, I went back inside, returned the pen to the waiter and myself to Grace. Mycroft eyed me suspiciously but continued our conversation at once.

"There are plenty of women here, Sherlock. The Diogenes Club prides itself on its policy of inclusion and non-gender-specific membership. One rule of the club, however, will always prevail, regardless of gender or personal pronoun."

He put a finger to his lips and beckoned us to follow. He led us in silence through the grand room, through a set of double doors and out into the back. We stopped and looked through a glass door into the infamous "Stranger's Room." It was absolutely heaving. Twenty maybe thirty women were packed in tight, drinking cocktails and talking nineteen to the dozen. Mycroft put his hands back in his pockets as he watched them. "Tonight, brothermine," he said, "sushi equals silence and I'm afraid as you can see, they would much rather starve. Feel free to jump in. You should be okay; I started piping oxygen in about an hour ago."

We went back inside. Lyra came to show us to our table, by which time my stomach was eating itself. I watched Mycroft slide outside to see what I had done to his sign and then concentrated on the wonderful creature that was sitting across from me. She was steaming slightly. I reached out and took her hands in mine.

"I am overjoyed you have come into my life, Grace. I know we will do something amazing together. Oh, and happy birthday."

CHAPTER FOUR

WHO CARES WINS

Apart from a few hours glued to the police scanner, gleaning what I could from the gruesome details that were coming over the radio about the previous night's events, I slept long and sound, no doubt owing in part to the mood I was in when I crawled into bed. I was over the moon that Grace was going to be in my life and though yes, there were times throughout the evening when I wanted nothing more than to just grab her and kiss her, I did resist and so, I'd like to think, did she.

The time we spent talking gave our meeting a more professional edge and my brother making a constant nuisance of himself served to dampen my ardor somewhat, though it wasn't a patch on the feeling I was getting from knowing that my initial feelings for her were without doubt given added impact, with the gulf between my expectation of her and how she really was.

Anyhow I put her in a cab back to Notting Hill and we agreed to touch base the next day. It was still dark when I rose. I filled my Vape with Blueberry Kush and set the temperature. While I waited for it to heat up, I made my garlic/turmeric/ginger/honey/ lemon/warm water breakfast shot, knocked it back in one and brushed my teeth. I then took my Vape, grabbed my crossbow from the wall and settled down in my armchair for a bit of a think over target practice.

Probably mindful of his overzealous entrance the day before, Dr. Watson crept up my staircase two hours later, with barely a knock or scrape, turned the door handle softly and swung the door open. I heard him sigh, then inch across the living room in the dark with his hands full. He put his laptop on the side table and leaned across to open the curtains. I don't know why I did it, I guess I thought it would be funny. Who knows why I do these things? It's like a physical form of Tourette's, I suppose. I want to do something, I gauge the reaction, I go over the pros and cons and then the hellion in me goes ahead and does it anyway. As soon as he went to open the curtain, I fired a bolt into the wall behind him. I guessed he'd be upset and he didn't disappoint. Dr. Watson pulled not only the curtain off, but the rail down...he held his coffee up as he stumbled backwards, then went over the side table and landed against the wall, from where he proceeded to throw his coffee all over himself. Dr. Watson jumped to his feet in a hail of profanities.

"FUCKOFF, IT'S FIRST THING IN THE FUCKING MORNING!" he bellowed, wiping hot coffee from his clothes. "I'm so glad I don't live with you anymore. This is a brand-new shirt, you bellend. Been up all night sleeping again I suppose."

I ignored him, bounced to my feet and rested the crossbow on its plinth. For once he was wrong.

"Not a bit of it, Watson. I've had a wonderful night's sleep." I sat back down and puffed thoughtfully on my Vape. Dr. Watson stared at me with a mixture of disgust and disdain.

"And what the hell's that thing?" he asked. "I thought you'd given up.

I held it up for us both to admire. It was made in the

shape of a pipe, though completely transparent. "It's my Vipe. Engineer in Angel made it for me. You put your tobacco, or liquid, or whatever in here, just press the button to change mode, the element heats it to the perfect temperature, digital readout here, the ice reservoir cools it down as it travels up here and Robert is your father's brother, a safer, smoother (puff puff) though not altogether legal smoke, Watson. I'm waiting. I wonder where Mrs. Hudson is. What was it, a flat white?. MRS. HUDSON?"

Dr. Watson sat down at the dining table and opened his laptop. He sniffed up.

"Certainly, doesn't smell like tobacco," he said. "Smells more like whatever. I must say, Holmes, that I think your new regime with Grace will work wonders for you. I don't think the gym will last, or the yoga, but I think the diet and meditation will help immensely. He looked over at me. "Waiting for what?"

There was a sharp rap at the door. I flashed my eyebrows at the doctor and shouted, "Come in, inspector!"

The door opened and Inspector Lestrade entered in a bit of a state. He looked haunted. He wore the same clothes as yesterday, was unshaven, unwashed and unhurried. In his hand he carried a brown paper bag, which held something else though I was oblivious to what this was. He would show me soon enough, I thought. I motioned him to a chair. He folded himself into it and breathed a heavy sigh. He gathered his wits and started. "Morning, Sherlock, morning, Dr. Watson," he said. "If you knew it was me, then I take it you know why I'm here."

I jumped from my chair and started to prowl the room. "Yes," I replied, well, bits and bobs. Something was found in a drainage channel last night. A body I believe, or part of one. I caught some of it on the scanner last night. Why do you think it might interest me, inspector."

Lestrade visibly dropped again, as he went through the details for the umpteenth time. "Well, that's what we've got Sherlock...bits and bobs. From what we can tell, we think it's a Caucasian male, dismembered, bits of flesh, no clothing, no ID, no fingers or teeth, so little chance of getting any ID, no idea about the manner of death, nor the time of death. Most of it has been dissolved. The pathologist seems to think he's been cooked.

Dr. Watson coughed and wandered into view, hands in his pockets. "There are many ways to dissolve a body," he said. "Most of the things you find under your sink that contain strong acids will do the job over time, sulphuric or hydrochloric for example. But if you want to do it quickly, bases are better for hydrolyzing esters, like those found in fatty tissues...so a concentrated sodium hydroxide would be far more efficient." I went back to my Vipe. "There you are, Lestrade," I said. "There's your answer. Well done, Watson. We've knocked one out before breakfast, if you'll pardon the expression, inspector. He hasn't been cooked at all; he's simply been dissolved."

The inspector looked weary. He took a plastic bag from the brown paper bag he was holding and held it up.

"With thyme and bay leaves?" he said.

I froze and shot a look at Dr. Watson. I was about to answer when Mrs. Hudson barged through the front door, covered in shopping. Leaving the door open, she zipped across to the fridge and began her daily activity of fitting half of Sainsbury's into it, while giving us a running commentary.

"I managed to get a refund on the barley miso," she informed me. "Then I went to Holland and Barret and got the white miso on a deal. If you spend forty-five quid on a jar of Manuka honey, you get the miso paste for free. Well, you know what I'm like for a bargain."

There wasn't any point in answering her as she wasn't

listening and even if she was, I knew nothing was being written to the hard drive. I ignored everything she said and kept my eyes fixed on the front door, which was still open. Mrs. Hudson finally caught on and excused herself on the spot. She hurriedly squeezed the remaining articles into the fridge.

"Oh, God, I've left the door open," she said. "I knew I was forgetting something. I've got a memory like a...like a...like one of those things you drain carrots with."

She rushed back over to the door and almost closed it on the woman she had left in the hallway. Mrs. Hudson started to unravel when she saw her and addressed our stranded guest with a heavy mixture of sadness and surprise. It was terrible to see her mind escaping her just from a personal standpoint, but to see the reaction play out on her face as it was happening to her was truly heartbreaking. I gave Mrs. Hudson a breather and sent her on a tea run, while I digested the imperious stature of the woman who had just walked through my door.

I had tracked two sets of heavy footsteps coming up the staircase and had easily deduced that one set belonged to a grocery-laden Mrs. Hudson. The other set, while obviously made by a larger person, were in no way confident steps committed to their action. The click of a low heel was quickly dulled by the careful planting of the foot and gave the effect that though the job of the step was to disperse weight evenly throughout the legs, each one gave me instead the distinct impression that they were painful steps and that this was somebody who desperately needed to take the weight off them altogether.

I caught the wave of an expensive heavy winter scent, straight from the souk in Dubai mixed with rubbing alcohol and soft notes of lint, and as she moved her frame subtly from one foot to another, I jumped to my feet and bid the shadow education secretary, Ms. Ellie-Mae Price and her injured legs to sit down.

I made a quick scan of her and while I introduced Dr. Watson and Inspector Lestrade, I made some more deductions. She was an unreasonable looking woman and was obviously trying her best to look distinguished, though quite clearly not enough time had been taken to this end. Her old Jaeger trouser suit was so ill-fitting, as to be either it's first time on, or had been borrowed from somebody else. Whichever it was, it hadn't been tried on first and was worn without ease or comfort besides. Nor had it been worn in order to project the idea of a powerful businesswoman, as that image would be impossible to avoid, no matter her attire. No, the trouser suit had been donned just for this occasion and more specifically to hide the injuries to her legs, unless of course I had bumped into someone else who was pretending to have injured legs. The overall ensemble had evidently been thrown together by someone not only in a rush, but quite clearly in a blind panic.

Her hair had succumbed to decades of chemical attacks and was now out of all style, shape or substance and was not so much fashioned and teased into shape but rather clawed back and bullied into a ratty bagel on top. Mutton dressed as mutton. The size of her forehead particularly drew my attention and without losing focus of her story, I calculated that on a clear day with no wind, I could probably put a bolt in it from three hundred yards with my crossbow. Couldn't miss if I tried. This idea was still in swaddling clothes when I noticed her eyes, and they troubled me to all distraction.

She had questiony eyebrows that dived to a point whenever anyone was talking and gave her an immediate air of suspicion and gave me the impression that even before I spoke that she didn't believe me and though fretted with fear for now, her eyes were grey and cold and cruel and looked like they had told many lies and seen many terrible things. Worse than that, they looked like eyes that had only ever sparkled when they had seen such things. They were eyes that stared out and watched on... eyes that watched on and did nothing. I didn't like her one bit, though right now I didn't know exactly why. I chastised myself for taking such a robust dislike to the woman but quickly recalled that I only knew who she was in the first place, due to a parliamentary memo I had caught a few weeks before. The Child Protection Bill was to be suspended due to covid restrictions and illness among its members and Ms. Price being one such member and more importantly, one that was planning to vote against the bill in its entirety, I was curious to know why. She eased herself into the armchair opposite and placed her hands on her knees. The thunderous voice I had heard her scare the House of Commons half to death with had gone and there was both genuine fear and confusion in it when she began.

"I would like to report an abduction," she said.

My heart sank. I jumped to my feet, instantly bored. I had much better things to do with my day. I motioned Inspector Lestrade towards her and then towards the door. "One for you, Lestrade," I said. "Thank you, Ms. Price, but I'm afraid that my taste in cases tends to run to the more, shall we say, exotic."

The inspector rose from his window seat and began to coax her from the armchair. "If you would like to accompany me down to the station, Ms. Price, we'll soon get to the bottom of this. Now, who's abduction exactly?"

She took a deep breath, during which time all eyes in the room turned on her. Excitement began to rise in me. I had no idea what she was going to say, but I knew it was going to be good and she didn't disappoint. Those steely black circles softened and began to well with tears. She blinked them back, wiped her face with the back of her hand and looked up at the inspector.

"Mine," she said.

Inspector Lestrade glazed over immediately. He was far too tired for this. He let out a groan of anguish and headed for the door.

"Ooooo...one for you, Sherlock. I'll meet you down at the morgue. Shall we say about an hour?"

I ignored the inspector and retook my place in the armchair, suddenly intrigued. Dr. Watson took his notebook and pen from his pocket and sat down. The minister gave us each one more plaintive glance with eyes that were soft and lost, then focused on a point on the rug on the floor between us and the coldness came back as she began to tell us her story. Ten minutes later, she breathed deeply again, blew out her cheeks and settled back in the chair. I hadn't taken my eyes off her throughout, looking for anything and everything where she might flounder, trip herself up or catch herself in a lie, but she never did. I wanted to believe her story, though it sounded too far-fetched. Something unnerved me about her, and I think that was the reason for my disbelief, but if she was telling the truth, then I might have got myself into something quite special. It couldn't be, could it? I had more questions for her and tried to remain composed. Secretly though, I couldn't stay inside my skin. As subtle as a chainsaw, I began my interrogation.

"You say he was a perfect gentleman. Tell me, Ms. Price... you weren't interfered with in any way?"

The minister stiffened at the thought, though I, I assure you, did not.

"No," she said. "There was nothing remotely sexual, or even sensual. There was something else though. I heard screams. But they were men, roaring in agony, like animals. An awful sound."

"So, there were others," I interjected, "Or have been

others. And not just women. And obviously you haven't been starved."

Dr. Watson cleared his throat and jumped in here. He started to read from his notes. "Well in fact, you said yourself, that it was quite the opposite. You were fed very well...amazing food, you said. "Chocolates, caviar."

The minister nodded in agreement. I got the feeling she was telling the truth as best she knew it. "I had a Sunday roast, my favorite movies and TV shows. And he had beautiful manners. Like I was in a dream."

I got to my feet and started to pace the room. "And how do you know that it wasn't a dream?"

She wrung her hands and let out a sigh. "It couldn't have been," she said.

Dr. Watson had heard enough. He put his notebook away and moved, as to shepherd her from the room.

"Ms. Price," he said, taking her elbow, "I implore you to present your case to Scotland Yard. Say I sent you. I'm sure they will give it their full attention. In the meantime, should anyone try to buy you a car for Christmas, or get you tickets for Ascot, you will be sure to let us know, won't you?"

I almost laughed out loud. The minister shrugged the doctor's hand away and turned again to me. The steel in her voice had returned.

"Ten days, Mr. Holmes. Ten days and I remember every single one clearly. I don't know what else to tell you. I have been held somewhere for ten days. I know I have. It was not a dream.

My mood was beginning to slip. I stopped pacing and stared down at her.

"Last week, I saw on a circuit memo, that you had contracted covid and had been forced to quarantine, day ten now I believe, which is how I recognized you when you first came in. The Child Protection Bill vote had to be postponed, as I recall. A bill that you opposed, I might add. I have been waiting for you to mention it. So, I do know that you have been away from parliament for ten days. But have you been missing from your house, I wonder."

Dr. Watson hovered over her, still trying to get her to her feet.

"There you are, you see," he said. "Had your jabs, have you? Booster, was it? Probably got one of those Chinese ones by mistake, made you hallucinate. They should stick to food and fireworks...and Kung Fu."

Ms. Price wasn't taking no for an answer. She waved away the good doctor yet again. "You're right, of course. I have had covid and yes, it is day ten now. I didn't think you would see me. I have been self-isolating for the last ten days and I have checked my CCTV over and over again. It shows quite clearly, Mr. Holmes, that I never left the house."

We were getting close; I could feel it. "Oh, I don't believe you did leave the house, or the cameras would have picked it up. I'm afraid, Ms. Price, that Dr. Watson is perfectly correct in what he says. You are obviously suffering some side effects from the vaccination. The injection has made you slip into a kind of dream-ravaged delirium of some sort. God knows I've had a few of those myself."

With that, the minister gave me a look of sadness and slowly started to take her shoes off. She delicately rolled up her trouser legs and pointed her toes. Her legs and feet were scratched to buggery. She looked at them and then at me.

"Are you dreaming these with me, Mr. Holmes?"

I stared at her legs. She then took the bag from beside the chair and brought from it a long tattered white dress."

"And when I woke up this morning, I was wearing this. This dress isn't mine, Mr. Holmes...it's his."

I looked at the dress in her hands, then back at her. I looked at the scratches on her legs and feet and then at the floor, then at Dr. Watson, then back at her. My senses began to swim. I felt like Sam Neill in Jurassic Park, when told by the park ranger that they had a T-Rex. My knees were weak and my legs started to give way. I put my hands on my knees and started to take deep breaths. Dr. Watson began to usher Ms. Price from the room.

"Thank you, Ms. Price," I said, "I will be in touch later today with my decision. Please leave the dress."

Dr. Watson saw the minister to the front door and by the time he had returned, I had almost pulled myself together. I fell into my chair and covered my eyes with my hands. It was important that I marshalled my thoughts as best I could before I spoke again, as my brain had just skateboarded off the end of the universe. Dr. Watson plonked himself in the chair opposite, stared at me and waited. In time, my thoughts became less nebulous, and I finally felt able to speak. I peeked at the doctor through my fingers.

"Watson, I think I'm high."

This wasn't what Dr. Watson wanted to hear. He snorted in derision, made a grab at a newspaper on the desk and aggressively began to read it.

"Probably that stupid contraption you're smoking out of," he remarked. "Probably got lead in it, or mercury...probably Chinese as well. Engineer in Angel my arse."

I continued. "No, you don't understand. I'm high on the situation.

CHAPTER FIVE

A DIVINE PROTOTYPE

"Watson, whatever forces of nature have combined to bring those two cases here together, now, is so improbable, it's impossible. But they are here now, so it can't be impossible. They are here for a reason...and the only reason I can think of..."

"Is the one that it can't be, obviously," the doctor offered unhelpfully.

"Exactly!"

"Which is?"

Excitement began to surge through me. I jumped to my feet and started to stride about the room without direction or purpose. I could hardly think what to do with this information. I stopped and looked at Dr. Watson, who was viewing my antics with amusement.

"But it can't be," was all I could come up with. "It's impossible. Watson, the game is afoot, or the games are afoot, or afeet. Watson, the games are afeet. Give me a minute, let me think...no, don't let me think, let me get dressed."

I continued to zoom about, this time full of purpose, though still lacking in any direction and not so much got dressed, as found garments of familiar shapes and attached them to matching parts of my body. My esteemed friend apparently hadn't caught on to the magnitude of what I was telling him. He shook his newspaper and glared ferociously at the words therein.

"Well, you can count me out," he spluttered. "I'm not going anywhere. I have a podcast to prepare. And it would be nice if you could show your face for once, Sherlock. These are your fans."

I couldn't believe my ears. I turned on him sharply.

"You want some syrup with that waffle, Watson...count you out? If this case is half as exciting as I think it is, then this will be our Magna Opera. They are your fans too. This will be the case that immortalizes us both.... *both* being the operative word." I flashed my eyes mischievously at him. "Thought of the answer yet?" The doctor remained unruffled.

"What, the answer that it can't be? No, Sherlock, I haven't. To be honest, since your little crossbow moment, I have been racking my brains for ways to dissolve a human body and I am coming up with new ways all the time, and until my coffee situation has been put to rights, I'm not going to think about anything else either. I'm going nowhere." I wasn't listening. I wasn't dressed either, in the conventional sense of the word. I went through my nest of socks and found a couple without holes in, then jumped into my shoes et voila, apart from my hands and face, I was covered and ready to go. I grabbed my Vipe and stood by the window, with my head full of magic.

"I'm talking of both. Both of what, you ask...both suggests two. So, two of what? Well, two of anything; in fact, two of everything. The duality of life, Watson, is what I'm talking about. We appear to have only one sun, though we do indeed inhabit a binary star system. The dwarf star, Nemesis, is our sun's dead twin and at the present time is being dragged around the sky by another planet. And here we are, Watson with two cases, both totally original concepts and unique to us as a team." I turned to him. "Now would I be right in saying, that in all our time together and all the cases we have solved, we have never had a cannibal or a time-traveler in any of them, in any form. Am I correct?"

Dr Watson started to fold his paper and take a bit more interest. He gestured his assent.

"Not that I can recall."

"So, let us take these two unlikely occurrences happening at all, at anytime, anywhere to anybody? Now what are the chances of them happening together, on the same morning, in the same room, with the same people present, in the same part of London? What does that tell you about my method, Watson."

Eager now to play a part, Dr. Watson cleared his throat and folded his hands together. "Well, what we normally do, is take away whatever is impossible and what we have left, no matter how improbable, is the answer."

And here is where I got excited. I started to pace the room again. "But not this time!" I exclaimed. "Here we have the exception to the rule. We have taken away the impossible, but what we are left with is more improbable than the impossibility we have just removed. By doubling the odds of probability and the chances of it now happening twice, we have created another world where it is now not only possible, but very highly probable. A set of circumstances so unlikely that they fail their own design. Two cases so unique, presenting themselves in such a way, can only mean one thing."

I stopped. Dr. Watson looked up at me like a puppy. He had an answer and at once looked quite proud of himself, though he didn't say it out loud for fear of being wrong. I could tell by his face that he wasn't wrong. I smiled broadly at him.

"Come on, Watson, you're almost there."

"But it can't be. Besides, things come in threes."

"No, they don't. They come in twos and while you are waiting around for the third one, you have already missed the message. Coincidences aren't chance happenings, they are exactly that...co-incidents. The same things happening at the same time, like coconspirators, co-operative, co-accused."

"But it's impossible."

I grabbed my overcoat from the hat stand and my hat from the coat rack and made for the front door.

"I know...don't you love it," I shouted as I left.... "Get your coat on, Watson, we're off to the morgue."

The reader will be aware by now that I had concluded that the person responsible for the body in the drain and the person who had taken Ms. Price hostage and had apparently taken others, was very much one and the same. Now it wouldn't be my first dealing with a serial killer, but one who cooked and possibly ate his victims, while not as uncommon as you would think, was a first for me. What made this one unique out of hand, not only to my case file, but to the world's at large, was the mind-blowing fact that this person, if indeed that's what they were, were able to be in two places at once and at the same time no place at all. We were dealing with an entity who could travel between dimensions and, as I stormed over the footbridge at Greenwich, I stopped dead. With a mixture of pure excitement and utter dread, I realized that the individual I had set my sights on was not of this world.

Serial killers I have found come in many shapes and sizes but evolve only in a few different ways. Very few of them intentionally set out to off as many people as they can, but they inevitably all start with their first kill. This act, as the reader will understand, is carried out for any one of the innumerable reasons that there are, of why one person would take the life of another. What happens after that is potentially where a serial killer is born. Let's take the first example. One person wants to take the life of another just to know what it feels like, kills, likes it and takes it from there. Another might unintentionally kill somebody and unexpectedly get some kind of thrill from it, be it a surge of power and having the fate of somebody's life in their hands, or is more often than not the case, they get some sexual gratification from it. Whatever the reason to start, in an equation with many variables, there is one common denominator that drives the urge to repeat the offence and that is the lack of consequence. There is not one day of difference in prison time for the person who takes the life of one and the person who shoots everyone in town. Why not carry on? Why not get better at it? Why not make a game of it? The decision to continue on that path isn't reduced to a question of why, but very much of why not.

This felt different though and not solely because of the seemingly supernatural identity of the assailant. If the cases as I suspected were connected, then this had all the hallmarks of retribution on an unimaginable scale. First up we have the victims. For the sake of argument, we will put Ms. Price for now into this category. Though she says she escaped, I am quite positive that she was allowed to leave for a reason and could have been dispatched at any time. Something told me that she, to the killer, was unfinished business.

Inspector Lestrade was already at the coroner's office by the time Dr. Watson and I had arrived and was involved in deep discussion with him. Dr. Watson made a grab for his handkerchief and gagged into it, as we contemplated the sinewy chopped up mess in front of us. A sullen mortuary assistant skulked about in the background. He looked familiar, though for right now I couldn't put my finger on the reason why.

I began to study the remains. The head and the torso were still barely attached. Tattered flesh still clung to parts of the skull and next to it were what I guessed to be the arms, the bones of which started off well, but faded to mush before the wrist. A pile of larger bones below the body, looked at first glance like the vertebrae of a larger animal, though on closer inspection turned out to be the perfectly sliced legs of the owner. I was about to ask the pathologist what the hell we had in front of us, but I couldn't seem to form the words...I didn't need to, no doubt my eyes were asking the same question. Inspector Lestrade pulled up a chair, as the pathologist took a chart from his desk and turned to me. He blew his cheeks out.

"A mixed bag really, Sherlock. I don't know what to make of it; there's a lot going on. Seems to be a mix of precision pathology and pathological psychopathy. The body seems to have been dissected with a high degree of finesse, even professionally I would say. No cut marks on the bones where the flesh was removed, though for some reason the upper legs seem to have been shattered with something heavy. The blows to the bones suggest they were done while he was still alive. The shin bones have been sliced into three-inch discs, again pre-mortem. This man suffered, and then he suffered some more and from what I can tell, that may have been the whole point.

I immediately focused on the shin bones, which had been sliced into perfect discs. From my old kitchen days, I knew that roasting the bones of animals was an old French technique for making stocks and from there the mother sauces. The arms and legs had been shattered and sliced to release the collagen from the bones, creating a natural thickener for the dish. The theory that this guy had been cooked was looking solid and though I can confess now, I was too embarrassed to admit it at the time, that I thought he smelled quite nice. I had seen enough.

"Anything else?" I said.

The coroner was already on it. "Best 'til last," he replied.

He pointed out parts of the spine with his pen. "Upon examining the bones, I noticed these marks on the vertebrae and the tailbone. There are several sets of them, all running the same way, up towards the skull. To mark the bones like this, serious force would need to have been used. The mark furthest up the spine is here, at the base of the neck. I have taken samples and the spectroscope is coming back with a high reading of silver. This man has had a silver spike inserted into his back passage, six or seven times with extreme violence. The coroner looked at each of us in turn over his glasses, as that information sank in. To hammer home the point, he added.

"If there isn't a sexually sadistic theme to this, I'd be very surprised. Even so, this goes way beyond any hurt or human suffering I have had before me, and all we have here, is a fraction of what actually happened."

Inspector Lestrade put his head into his hands with the air of a man who was suddenly re-evaluating his life. Dr. Watson looked on with eyes bulging, one hand still over his mouth. The inspector looked up.

"Would that have killed him?" he asked.

The coroner blew his cheeks out again. "Well, you would have hoped so, wouldn't you? It would have crashed his nervous system, and all brain activity would have ceased immediately, so if it didn't physically kill him, at least he wouldn't have been able to feel whatever fresh torment was coming next. I suspect most of the suffering came when he was still alive. Somebody really hated this guy."

I bent forward, inches from the remains and used every sense to take in as much detail as I could. I stopped just short of feeling sorry for the victim and what he had been through and moreover, what someone else had been through, in order for him to end up like this. I stared into the eye sockets.

"What did you do?" I said.

Stepping back onto the sticky, humid street proved no less

cloying than the stifling closeness of the morgue, but after breathing in a few scorched lungfuls of relatively fresh London air, I knew that I would get nothing out of Dr. Watson until he had his coffee and as we stood in the queue of some pseudo-Italian chain, I was careful not to direct any questions towards him, but instead spoke to myself with my face pointing towards him and just loud enough for him to hear; any participation on his behalf would be entirely voluntary.

"I don't get why she was unharmed," I pondered. "He obviously had plans for her. But what, if not sex? And what changed? There wasn't any ransom demand, so it wasn't a kidnapping. And why let her escape? He obviously changed his mind, but why? She said that none of the doors were locked, then she blacks out in a forest and wakes up in bed ten days later, with no memory of being in her own house, though the cameras prove she was there. We don't know where she was kept, why she was kept, and more importantly how she was kept, if she was quite clearly at home. Alternatively, we have an unidentifiable male, who has been tortured to death and turned into soup."

The woman in front of me turned around and stared at me, ushering her child out of earshot. I lowered my voice but moved closer to Dr. Watson and spoke directly into his ear.

"Do you believe in other dimensions, Watson?" I asked.

The doctor didn't even look at me. "Do they have coffee there? No, Sherlock, I don't."

Damn Watson's eyes. It was impossible to get anything resembling a conversation out of him until he had drunk his coffee. He didn't even need to drink it; he just needed to feel it in his hand. Psychosomatic again? This morning though he was being particularly difficult, as his coffee moment had been spoiled and I was entirely to blame. We reached the front of the queue. I didn't like his answer.

"You seem very sure," I said. "Do you agree that we see and hear things all the time, which are outside the range of human vision and hearing? Err, a flat white and a half-fat, decaf, skinny Frappuccino, less foam but more air in the foam."

The change in Dr. Watson, once he had his coffee in hand, was something to behold.

"Like a dog whistle, you mean?"

"In its simplest form, yes. But what about the other senses? Do you also agree that there are tastes and smells that human beings cannot discern, but other entities can?

And as such, can we agree that they also must exist."

Dr. Watson was putting the finishing touches to his coffee. "Stands to reason," he conceded.

"Well, what about touch?"

"What do you mean? You can't feel something that isn't there. Well, maybe the wind." I pushed on. "But can you touch something without feeling it? Or can something touch you without you feeling it? How do you know that it isn't there? If you can't see it, hear it, smell it or taste it, then that's fine, it can still exist. But if you can't touch it, then you can't?

We stepped back out into the fresh air. Dr. Watson checked the lid on his cup was secure.

"You're the one who mentioned touch," he said.

"Yes, but not just with your fingers. Think about feeling in a much broader sense. If something touches your heart, you feel it, do you get me? Think about feeling with everything."

After performing a couple of circuits of it, I realized that Dr Watson was trying to keep the park bench between me and his coffee. I stopped and stared at him. He held his hand out towards me, as if to fend me off and raised the cup to his lips.

"You stay exactly where you are," he ordered.

After taking a few dramatic slurps of his beverage, he

ambled round to the business side of the bench and we both sat down. He carried on where we had left off.

"What I'm going to think about, Sherlock, is getting back to work. I have a lot to do. What are you up to today?"

I wasn't really sure, so I told him what I thought he wanted to hear. "What I'd like to do this morning, is get hold of the CCTV from Ms. Price's apartment. Time is a human construct, Watson invented to measure change, but it can be manipulated, especially with cameras. We have to rule that out first. Then I'm going back to flat to have a look at that dress. Wanna come with?"

"Aren't you going to be late?"

"Late for what?"

"Your regime starts today," he said. "I thought you were going to yoga."

I laughed out loud. I had totally forgotten. "Bollocks to yoga," I said.

A text flashed up on my phone. It was from Grace and it said, "You are only cheating yourself."

I stared at my phone, turned it over in my hands, showed the message to Dr. Watson, then looked behind me and made a quick scan of the small park. "How did she do that?

Can she hear me? See me? It hasn't even started yet," I protested.

The good doctor was finally finding his groove. The change in him after a couple of sips of coffee was remarkable and I felt that I wanted to raise the subject of psychosomatics and the placebo effect again. Instantly I thought better of it, as I didn't want to spoil his mood, so I stayed quiet and resolved to switch out his multishot flat white for a decaffeinated substitute later in the week and monitor the results.

"Women's intuition, Holmes."

"Exactly, Watson," I exclaimed. "The perfect example of feeling without touch. It's all about the gut brain and the

HPA axis. The hypothalamus, pituitary and adrenalin glands are all linked by a neurological highway, the one that controls your gut instinct, your fight or flight mechanism, your sixth sense. I'm going to be learning about it all in my class."

Dr. Watson smiled and nodded. He had cheered up and speeded up and was ready to engage. Real or imagined, I silently thanked his coffee for its help.

"Okay, well I'll tell you what. Seeing as it isn't a good idea to start off on a bad footing with Grace, I suggest that you get yourself along to the gym and I'll get Ms. Price to send us the CCTV footage, and we can go through it when you get back."

Defeat came quickly. I sighed, got to my feet and threw my coffee in the bin.

"Okay, okay, I'll go. I'm supposed to be drinking tea anyway." I thrust my hands deep into my pockets and stared morosely at the list of dos and don'ts from Grace, that was scrolling inside my head. Dr. Watson got to his feet, and we began to exit the park. "I'm not allowed any processed foods either," I added, and only high-alkaline foods at that. The gut brain needs to work. Apparently, it's the number one brain and more important than the one we carry around up here."

This information was music to the doctor's ears. The thought of me taking medical advice from someone cheered him up no end. He smiled broadly at me, as we exited the park.

"I'm glad you have finally seen reason, Holmes, and are really going to take her advice."

"I'll be eating a lot of raw food as well. No more dead food. It's about eating enzymes, Watson, life on a plate. And I'm not really taking anybody's advice. What have I told you about that? Good advice is never to be taken, it's only to be passed on. I will give you the benefit of the doubt here as this advice is...." I stopped dead in my tracks, frozen with excitement. Dr. Watson stopped too and stared at me with mild amusement.

"Watson, I've got it!" I spluttered. "Of course. It's been staring me in the face. I was right. We were right. Life on a plate! Watson, if you were going to keep somebody against their will, apart from kidnapping them, or for sex, what is the one reason that you would keep someone relaxed and not stress them out and damage their flesh?" The doctor stared at me.

"I have no idea," he said.

I took several deep breaths before I was able to answer.

"If you were going to eat them," I said. "He's cooking the men, though I don't know if he's eating them. He isn't hurting the women, because he isn't cooking them." I looked deep into Dr. Watson's eyes and smiled. "He's eating them raw."

Dr. Watson's jaw dropped as he digested this news. He finally closed it and pushed some words out. "If I didn't know any better, I would say that this sounds like Moriarty," he said.

It had started to rain. I turned my face to the sky. "Oh, we are going to wish it was....no, doctor," I replied, "this is much, much worse."

We stood at the park gates, ready to go in different directions. Dr. Watson looked at me suddenly seriously. "And how do you suggest we go about finding him?"

I looked to the sky again, the rain now hammering down on my face. No matter the weather; bring the cold and the wind while you're at it; I didn't care, I felt joy in my heart, I felt meaning and purpose. I felt value and worth. More than this, I felt chosen. My heart sang. "We don't have to," I said turning on my heel and marching off into the crowds, leaving Dr. Watson staring after me, "he has already found us! I'll see you later!"

CHAPTER SIX

DORIAN

My rare, good night's sleep had done me the power of good. My limbs felt long and loose and there was a smoothness to my stride, which was usually an achy mechanical stomp. It was the only encouragement I needed to cancel my yoga class. A conversation with Grace would have no doubt given her the chance to talk me into it and this morning, though I was gliding around London's shimmering streets with unnerving aplomb, I didn't quite have enough confidence not to buckle under the slightest pressure from her, so I sent her a quick text and then pretended not to hear the beep of her immediate (and no doubt disappointed) response. I needed to think and to do that, I needed to walk.

From Greenwich, I made my way over the Blackwall Tunnel bridge, across the Isle of Dogs and had arrived in Canary Wharf and was on towards Limehouse way before I had expected to be. I was loving my new walking style, but it was a bit too quick for me. I had more thinking left to do than I had steps left to Baker St, so I crisscrossed the river at every bridge and with the turgid River Thames grinding its way through the city beside me, I reached Waterloo, then struck out through Picadilly and Soho towards my flat. As I came up the stairs, I distinctly heard the words microchip and injection coming from Dr. Watson and I knew I was right to get my thinking out of the way, before I got home.

"It's called a jab nowadays," I corrected the doctor, as I stood there, dripping wet and smiling from ear to ear. "The government won't use the word, injection...too much stigma attached. It conjures up the image of heroin addicts, like me!"

Dr. Watson was seated at the breakfast table with his laptop. Mrs. Hudson started to make herself look busy and then made herself scarce. There was a parcel on the table that I knew was for me, just by the very fact that it remained unopened. I crooked my neck at the delivery note attached and started slowly to circle the table.

"Anything on Ms. Price's CCTV, Watson?" I asked.

"She sent it about five minutes ago, I haven't opened it yet," he replied.

I picked up the box from the table, smelled it, shook it and put it to my ear, then sat in my armchair, placed the package on my knee and stared at it. Dr. Watson stopped what he was doing and turned to me.

"Do you want to have a look at the dress while I get the file ready?"

I smiled at the doctor. "I don't think so." "I believe that all our answers are right here in this box."

With that, I got back to my feet, put the parcel back on the table and removed my pocketknife.

"Looks suspicious," the doctor exclaimed. "Do you want me to get in touch with Lestrade, to secure the box for fibers and prints and such?"

I retrieved my magnifying glass from my desk and sized up the box. "There won't be any." I bent over the package and began to study it. I had noticed that there was a small flattened out, face-down small pile of cardboard, sitting on the table, which meant that somebody else had received a parcel besides me and on the floor, on the way to the bin under the sink, were four tiny polystyrene balls. I put this together with the conversation I had just walked in on and knew that if only I could be bothered to open the door of the fridge, then I would see the vials of poison that Watson intended to stick in me on the government's behalf had arrived.

"Handwriting, Watson," I said, "can tell much more about a person than what their writing is like. It looks very much like an old copperplate hand, which unless is a hobby, was only practiced in schools many years ago and would put the writer of it well into their seventies. Two reasons why this isn't the case...copperplate has a slant to the right, whereas this is practically vertical. We can also rule that out, as you would expect to see a shake in the hand of someone of that age, a twitch, signs of rheumatism...not a trace, not one mistake. Every letter is smooth and sure. This isn't your weekend calligrapher either, as the letters aren't written separately, they flow one into another. No, this is this person's actual handwriting. When was the last time you wrote something, Watson? Exactly. I know people who have forgotten how to write altogether. The writer of this text is keeping the discipline alive. He's principled, meticulous, confident, adventurous and supremely intelligent."

I put my magnifying glass down and opened the blade on my knife, then quickly cut the tape down the center of the box and gave Dr Watson a manic smile. "I can't wait to meet him," I said.

Mrs. Hudson reappeared but stood and watched the proceedings from the safety of the doorway. Dr. Watson strained his neck to see, as I unfolded the flaps of the box and peered inside. I gently reached in and lifted the contents out and set them on the table. It was a VR headset, of all things. I picked it up and peered into the goggle end, then turned it over in my hands a few times, to make sure it wasn't booby-trapped. I found the strap and with a brief glance at Mrs. Hudson and the good doctor, I slowly slipped it over my head and pressed the "on" button.

The screen was black. A golden seven-pointed emblem appeared in the center of it and slowly started to turn, like the inner workings of a Franck Muller watch. The wheels and cogs began to spin on their own axes and then exploded in slow motion and every part started to spin by itself. A handsome, elegant-looking man appeared, sitting in a black leather reclining chair. He was dressed immaculately. He stood and started to walk around, then stopped and addressed the camera.

"Hello, Sherlock," he said, "my name is Dorian. As you are aware, everything that exists lives on vibration; the vibration of things tells of their virtues and their vices. Vibration and magnetism are the source of all life and changes with every single thought. All negative vibrations are toxic, so the moment a person becomes envious, hateful or greedy, the light around them changes and the magnetic field around them is damaged. Good thoughts and good actions make every cell in the human body feel better, because the magnetic field is wrapping them in light. But with bad thoughts and bad decisions, sometimes we must turn on the dark."

The view on the screen changed and suddenly we were in a different room, a dark, forbidding-looking room, with the walls and the floor being bare rock. I couldn't make anything out to begin with, apart from a small wood fire in the center of the room. There was muttering coming from somewhere and as my eyes adjusted to the gloom, I was met with a terrible sight.

A few meters away from the fire, stood what I knew to be from my studies on Ancient Rome, a large brass bull, the Brazen Bull, one of the most terrifying instruments of torture the human race was ever to conceive. It had been fitted with wheels and a door that opened in the animal's near side. The muttering turned out to be coming from an old white-haired man, who was strapped to a post on the other side of the fire, with his hands tied behind him. His face was turned upwards, as if offering prayers, or beseeching the heavens. He was naked apart from a garment of underwear. Away towards the back of this cavern came a loud hiss. A door opened in the wall and Dorian, the man who had just addressed me, entered slowly.

Before me this time however, stood not the debonair, beguiling soul from before. Oh no. It was without a doubt the same person, but this time he looked truly terrifying. He wore a black kimono, which he discarded to reveal a lean, ripped torso painted heavily with hieroglyphs. He stopped and stared at his captive, his eyes dark and soulless, his mouth drawn into a malevolent sneer. He started to walk towards the old man and addressed him in a voice that came from Lucifer himself.

"Organized religion," he snarled. "The very essence of Sado-masochism...the master and slave relationship." He moved closer to the old man, now their faces almost touching. "Being forced to love *someone you fear!"* he screamed. The old man started to whimper again; his eyes turned toward the heavens again. Dorian smiled at the prostrate captive and put his nose to the air.

"I can smell your soul, Oh man of God. Do you fear me?" he asked.

The priest screwed his eyes up, then nodded frantically. Dorian didn't look convinced. His face fell. "But you don't love me," he continued. The captive, who I assumed now to be a priest, shook his head, thought better of it and nodded furiously again. Dorian laughed and began to walk purposefully around him.

"I understand, you are confused," he said. "Obviously, you can't love me. Maybe I should force you to."

He rammed his face right up into the face of his gibbering

guest. "Do you know why you're here, man of God? *Open your fucking eyes! Do you know why you're here?"*

The priest kept his eyes firmly shut, shook his head weakly and began to cry. His tormentor walked quickly across to a table that I hadn't yet seen, as it was draped with a large black cloth. He pulled the cloth back to reveal an impressive range of tools and surgical instruments. Though I couldn't make out exactly what, he took a small silver tool, that may have been scissors. I jumped a little as the camera suddenly zoomed in. He took a black Velcro strap and fastened the priests head to the post. He then took a pair of long-nosed pliers, which he attached to the eyelashes and pulled down one of the priest's eyelids. He then produced a pair of curved scissors with the other hand, reached up and swiftly cut off the priest's eyelid. The priest let out a bloodcurdling scream and opened his other eye wide.

"It's open, it's open!" he yelled.

Dorian drew his head back and looked at the priest. "Yeah, but now you look strange. It's weird when you blink. Let's even it up."

With that, he reached out and performed the same process with the other eyelid. The priest continued to scream, his head straining against the post and blood streaming from his eyes. Dorian stepped back to admire his handiwork, then spoke in a more measured tone.

"Oh, I know you're sorry," he said. Faced with their crimes, most people are. I heard you muttering when I came in. Think he's going to save you? Do you think that after forty years of raping children, he's just going to jump in at the last minute? You think he approves? You do know it isn't worship, it's workship...you work for your God. This is you doing his work, is it? He's not going to save you. I think he's going to do exactly what he did with your victims. I think he's going to stand by and watch. Let's give him a show. Stick your tongue out."

The priest's mouth remained firmly shut. Dorian walked across to the fire, took a burning piece of wood from it and put it to the wispy patch of hair that the priest had left. It went up instantly, fizzing and crackling. The flames went out quickly and the priest's screams dropped to a whimper. His head smoldered. Dorian put his face close and addressed him again.

"You may have gathered by now, that I'm not a big fan of repeating myself," he said "now, stick your tongue out, or I'll go in and get it."

He then went back across and took a glowing iron from the fire and a block of wood from the table. He presented himself again before the distraught priest.

"Right, tongue out....out...a bit more...a bit more."

Quick as a flash, Dorian put the wooden block under the priest's tongue and pressed the iron against it from above. A strangled, unearthly howl emanated from the priest, who then collapsed in shock, his head dropped onto his chest, eyes forever wide open. Dorian went across to the brass bull.

"As much as I'd love to spend all day listening to you scream, with this instrument it doesn't really have the same effect," he said. I suppose you've seen one of these before, though I've modified it for your benefit." He turned to the priest and his face fell.

"Oh, you've fallen asleep," he remarked, "am I boring you?"

With that Dorian went back over to the table, took a large pair of shears and without a second's thought, strode over to the priest and deftly cuts one of his nipples off. The priest screamed himself awake again and looked wildly about for an escape. His tongue had started to swell, and his screams were getting less human-like. Dorian smiled and went in close.

"Sorry about that, you nodded off. Am I keeping you up? I don't want you to miss this. I've gone to a lot of trouble. How's the tongue? Oh, that's perfect."

He then went to a corner of the room and came back with an armful of wood that he put directly onto the fire. He then reached behind the priest and unscrewed a clamp in the middle of the frame. He pushed the priest back and refastened the clamp. The priest was now horizontal, facing up and then pushed the bull into position behind him. He opened the door in the side of the bull and hauled the priest across, still attached to the pole. He was now lying inside the cavity of the bull. He cut away the priest's underwear and threw it into the fire also.

"Hurting those you have sworn to protect," he said. "Abusing those who put their trust in you. The damage. *The damage you have caused* cannot possibly be repaired in one lifetime, so your suffering will not stop here. It will go on and on and every pointless remake of your miserable fucking soul will suffer in the same way. The pain that you are about to feel, will be the pain you will carry forever." Dorian looked the priest in his blooded eyes and smiled.

"Starting now!"

With that, he grabbed a handle attached to the post, turned it and the priest flipped over. Dorian closed the door and wheeled the bull into the fire. A deep bellowing started to come from the bull. Dorian started to play an invisible theremin and turned and walked towards the camera, towards me and stopped, still appreciating the noise coming from the brazen bull. He sang as he approached the camera. "Give me joy in my heart, keep me praising. Give me joy in my heart I pray." He stopped and smiled.

"I thought they said that nothing good ever came of the dark ages," he said. "I must say, great acoustics."

I laughed out loud and for a split second, forgot where I

was. In that short time, the image on the screen had changed and once again I saw the exploded insignia and the Dorian I had seen before had returned. I must say I much preferred this version of him, though I scolded myself for rather taking to him. I wondered which part had been recorded, probably the death of the priest. I scolded myself for watching the events that had unfolded before me but found some comfort in the fact that it was necessary, if I had any hope of proceeding further with this case.

Dorian smiled and addressed me once more and, as if he knew what I had been thinking, said, "Don't be so hard on yourself, Sherlock; it was vital that you watched it. Don't worry, you will forget it soon enough."

I was thunderstruck. How did he do that? *I should ask him,* I thought. Before I could speak however, he put a finger to his lips and continued.

"One benefit of television, Sherlock, is the chance to see air as a conductor. We can watch all kinds of programs and flick from one to another, and the channel is held on its own course...like it has its own orbit. What you have just seen, for example, didn't take place in your apartment. It took place somewhere else and travelled unseen through the air to get to you and then re-assembled itself for your entertainment. Unfortunately, for your species, I'm afraid that the show is almost over. This Type One civilization has been erased twice before, and the planet is ready to claim what is rightfully hers. As I said, Sherlock, my name is Dorian and I represent the Council of Seven. I am your only chance, Sherlock, and you... are theirs. It will take an unusual mind to prevent this from happening, which is why I have chosen you. This planet is broken and it's up to you to fix it. If it wasn't such a puzzle, it wouldn't be you. Sadly, at this moment in time, you can't prevent anybody from dying, as examples must be made, but you can alter the outcome. You will make your own clues as you go along and every decision you make will generate more possibilities, but less answers and will lead you to, as you know, the only possible answer."

He then said something that froze my blood. "Put that brain of yours to good use, Sherlock," he said. He then motioned below, or downstairs in the basement and added, "before someone else does!"

The screen suddenly went black. I sat for a second, as my thoughts scrambled for a foothold, but just like the seven-pointed golden insignia I had seen, they threatened to come together and then exploded into smaller fragments and started to spin. Right at the very center of this mental vortex were the words, "before someone else does." I took off the headset and looked at Dr. Watson, who was staring me out of all countenance for an update.

"That was Dorian," I said. Mrs. Hudson and Dr. Watson waited for more information, but I didn't have any. Why did Dorian refer to himself as someone else? An alter-ego? Twin brother? However many of them there were, it did go a small way to my immediate deduction, that therein lay the answer to him being in two places at once. Dr. Watson had stared enough. He fidgeted in his seat, rummaging for a question. "Well, what is it, Holmes?" he ventured finally. "Is it a game?"

My brain had burst its banks. "Huh?" I said. "Here, see for yourself."

I passed the headset to him; he slipped it on and pressed the button, then took it off directly and passed it back. "Can't see a damn thing," he announced.

I took the headset from him and put it on again. Immediately I was presented with the fragmented golden star and as before, it exploded slowly are started to rotate. I took it off and passed it back to him.

"Here, look now," I said.

Dr. Watson went through the motions again, then yanked

it off and tossed it on to the table, evidently annoyed. "Not a sausage," he said.

With that, the doctor engaged himself once more with his work. I grabbed the headset again, put it on and talked him through what I was seeing.

"It's here!" I exclaimed...discs and spheres and a gold, seven-pointed star. It's all there. You didn't see any of this?"

Dr Watson was heavily engrossed in whatever was on his laptop screen.

"No, Sherlock, I didn't," he said. "Maybe this is a journey you have to go on by yourself. Like Frodo."

CHAPTER SEVEN

ON THE MENU

I stood and went to the window. Below me the traffic squirmed either way up Baker St like toothpaste. People shielded themselves from the rain, as they went about their important business, their life and death struggles, fulfilling their obligations, honoring their promises and making their deadlines. And all for what? Was it all really so important? To choke on fumes and be made deaf by noise? To be soaked to the skin and be freezing cold inside? To run, to worry and to never rest?

I had become acutely aware of the futility of existence; not so much mine, but of everyone else's. Would they appreciate it? Would they even notice? Why would I save them? These musings were brought into razor-sharp focus with the sobering knowledge, that if I didn't save them, then my own demise might not be as benign and uneventful as theirs. No, I had been singled out for special attention. I thought of the priest tied to the stake and saw myself there, begging for both mercy and instant death. I had a profound sense that I would get along very well with Dr. Jekyll, but how to stay out of the clutches of Mr. Hyde was the question. It seemed to me that this was something that even Dr. Jekyll couldn't guarantee.

The thing that frightened me even more than this though, was the disturbing thought that he could possibly know what I was thinking.

Mrs. Hudson in this time had been away to make tea, though came back empty-handed and started to tidy up instead. She stopped putting knives and forks away and for some reason looked very pleased with herself. She turned to me.

"So, what did this Dorian say?" she asked.

"Well, it's all very simple," I said. "I have a mystery to solve and a killer to catch...and if I don't, then it's the end of civilization...that old chestnut. And just for added spice, if I don't solve it, then I'm probably going to end up on the menu."

Mrs. Hudson looked over at me and pulled her face. "I don't think that's a very good idea," she said.

I must admit, I was a tiny bit offended. "What's that supposed to mean?" I asked, around my Vipe.

Undeterred, Mrs. Hudson picked at the scab and continued to hide my possessions around the flat. "Well, I wouldn't eat you," she said. "You're too stringy...you're like an impala. I mean you're a lovely looking lad and all. Mind you, I've got no room to talk... I'd take forever to cook...maybe eight hours on a low light...probably overnight."

Dr Watson and I exchanged glances, but I wasn't defeated just yet. I had taken the bizarre decision to defend myself as a cannibal's choice of entree.

"Well, I'm sure you'll be delighted to know that he isn't going to eat my body, just my brain," I parried.

Mrs. Hudson stopped for a second, then thrust again. "Ah," she said, "he's probably going to do a stir-fry, bit of mange touts, ponzu sauce, that'd be lovely."

"He probably won't be cooking me," I countered. "It seems to me, that he feeds on energy. I'll most probably be eaten raw." A thought struck me. "Maybe eaten alive," I added. "I could watch!"

Mrs. Hudson didn't bat an eyelid. "I was going to say," she said, "raw would be better. I'd do a nice carpaccio, thinly sliced, black radish, pink grapefruit, nice vinaigrette."

I was done. Clubbed into submission, I sat in stunned silence, completely astonished that such a seemingly harmless, genteel person could treat such an unsavory subject with this level of frivolity. Dr. Watson sprang to my aid. He looked over at me and tapped his temple with his finger.

"Have you been at the Tom Kerridge again, Mrs. Hudson?"

Mrs. Hudson stopped and straightened her pinny. "No, it's my new one," she said. "German fella...Otto Lenghi. Oh, by the way, I'm not cooking tonight, I'm out with the girls. I thought maybe we could have Chinese. You'll be alright with that, won't you, Sherlock? I mean it's only fried salad really."

I went to my mind palace and flicked through the pages of my international chef directory, looking firstly for German chefs, then American or British chefs with German-sounding names who were at least famous enough to write a recipe book. I highlighted Thomas Keller, Daniel Hummn and Wolfgang Puck, then scrapped them and prepared myself to step outside the box, seeing as this was Mrs. Hudson. An eruption of laughter from Dr. Watson derailed my train of thought right there and he rounded on us both with unabashed pride. I raised my eyebrows at him, though really at myself. Was I losing my touch?

"Yotam Ottolenghi is Israeli, I think," he interjected. Something on the laptop screen suddenly caught the doctor's attention. "Well, hello, Dorian," he exclaimed, staring at the screen with redoubled scrutiny. "There he is...or he was...well somebody was." I jumped from my chair and went over to hover at Dr. Watson's shoulder, as he zipped back and forth with the timeline on the screen.

"2:18am...4th of August...somebody or something arrives like lightning" he announced... "straight through the front door and straight out of the back. I can't make out what it is; it's just a shadow. I'll fast forward it to when she returns, even though as you can see, she quite clearly hasn't gone anywhere, maybe we can pull up a better image."

It was indeed as the good doctor described. No matter how much the video was slowed down, a dark shadow was seen to enter the front of the house and exit the rear at supernatural speed and though Ms. Price was lying on a sofa downstairs when the shadow both entered and left the premises, we were able to freeze the frame at certain points and then enlarge the image, to discover that whoever or whatever had passed through her house at that time of the morning, had also passed through her.

I refilled my Vipe and went back to my seat. I was still a little concerned that Dr. Watson had beaten me to the "German chef." Though I had never graced any of his establishments, the name was now familiar, but too familiar and too late. I now remembered that there were six such eateries under this chef's purview in London alone. I also remembered their addresses, their drinks menus and the names of all of their managers. Either my techniques were rubbing off on Dr. Watson and he was getting better, or my mental faculties were being compromised, and my abilities were in decline. Either way, my mood darkened, as I puffed morosely on my Vipe. The doctor broke into my gloom.

"Well, you saw him," he said. "What does he look like?"

It hit me suddenly that this was another question I had no definitive answer to, though the possibilities were mind-blowing. I had ruled out Dorian having an alter-ego, by him describing his other self-downstairs as "someone else." This left only us with the evil twin scenario, which I didn't mind, though with the introduction of inter-dimensional travel, we had given ourselves another possibility to consider. Let's say that these two, whoever they are...are from somewhere else and have taken over the physical body of somebody on Earth and could manifest at different times, as different entities... then what? Come on brain, what's happening? Do your stuff.

"There are two of them," I replied. "Unless there are two of him, in which case there are three of them."

Dr. Watson was still going through the footage. "And again August 13th 8.14pm," he remarked. "Same shadow, same speed. Ms. Price is right, something definitely happened to her, but I'm not even sure that's a human being."

For some reason my thinking was getting rather nebulous; I wasn't having any trouble bringing topics to mind, but from there on in, they scattered in all directions and refused to suffer further scrutiny. I held my Vipe up and stared at it. I was purposely staying away from the Indicas on offer; those I could only smoke in the evening, when all of my responsibilities had been taken care of. I put my Vipe in its holder and picked up the headset again.

"Ms. Price's movements are no longer any concern of ours, Watson," I said. "We have all we need to know. She was only used as bait to attract my attention. I have a feeling he'll be back for her."

Dr. Watson huffed and puffed a little, no doubt he wanted more from the CCTV. "Well, you can stop him, Holmes," he grunted.

"That's just the point, Watson. How do I stop him? You said yourself that he isn't human. I'm afraid that's all I'll ever be."

I picked up the headset and slipped it on again. Same dance, spheres and rings and a golden star all spinning slowly. I yanked it off and threw it into my backpack. For some reason my hair was sticky. My thinking was the same, something was wrong. I jammed my hat on my head, grabbed a dry coat and made for the front door.

"I'm going out for a bit," I said. "I need to skim the excess froth from my head."

The doctor wasn't happy about this. "So, what do you want me to do?" he protested. "We just sit back and wait for the next victim?"

I stopped short of the door, while I fastened my coat. "Well, there's no mystery about the next one," I said, "I don't know who he is, though I'm positive he's a priest; I'm sure if we check if any have gone missing in the last twenty-four hours, we'll find out soon enough, but I do know when, how and why he died."

Mrs. Hudson was putting a few finishing touches to the flat. "How do you know all that?" she asked.

"Because I've just watched it happen. I'll pick up Chinese on my way back." My mind went blank. "Where is it?"

They both looked over at me with some disbelief. Mrs. Hudson laughed. "Where is Frank Wong's? You've only been going for twenty years, Sherlock...right at the bottom of the..."

"Left at the bottom of the road!" Dr. Watson interrupted, "then first right...it's red and gold. I'll have Singapore noodles, if you can remember.... what do you mean, you've just watched it happen?"

I just stared at him. I had neither the time nor the enthusiasm to explain. I felt sick; I needed to breathe and I knew exactly where I could go to do that.

CHAPTER EIGHT

BROTHERMINE

I am certain that the reader will agree with me that the two most desperate problems ailing modern society are stress and anxiety on one hand and depression on the other, and the devastating problems they bring with them. To my mind, they occupy opposite sides of the same human experience and being wholly man-made, happily carry their own antidote and therefore, I believe, the solution to the problem.

To me depression is everything to do with the past...that failed marriage, the trip you didn't go on, the time you were afraid to ask, the one that got away...all regret, all revenge and all remorse lives here. Stress and anxiety sit at the other end of the human experience and is everything to do with the future...the car payment you can't make, the bully walking down the street towards you, or the sun eventually burning us to cinders.

The fear of what might be reduces us to gibbering wrecks and is caused by things that haven't yet happened, be they two minutes or ten thousand years from now. If we can agree that time is indeed a human construct, invented by mankind to measure change, then the obvious answer would be to live in the present, at all costs. This, however, brings with it a whole host of difficulties. Advanced planning in matters of work, health and family, and prudence in financial affairs is no doubt sensible advice and providing a secure future both for yourself and your offspring will undoubtedly reduce the amount of stress and anxiety that would surely come into your life, should you be lacking in such provision. Matthew Verse 6 Chapter 34 advises to "have no thought for the morrow," and while this might sound like a call to spend everything you have immediately and bugger the consequences, I rather like to look at this statement with a burgeoning Taoist heart, in so much as letting events and indeed all time before you unfold as it should, for things have happened, things will happen and no amount of money or medication is going to change anything.

So, it is in principle that I agree with long-term far-reaching changes to one's situation; what I am trying to eliminate from my life are matters of immediate pleasure, rapid reward and personal short-term highs. It is said that desire will only bring suffering, though I have now discovered that it's much worse than that.... desire *is* suffering. The very act of wanting more, the feeling of not being satisfied with what you have means you are already suffering and it's only going to get worse as you realize that every time you attain the thing you sought, it still isn't enough and sadly it never will be. Short-term pleasure, on the other hand, can be found elsewhere in other activities, can be completely ignored or with the help of Seneca and Marcus Aurelius in my case, can be faced and overcome.

Confronting the darkness in yourself makes it easier to see and sometimes understand the darkness in others and so that's the place I started. Most of the more nefarious hobbies and general bad practices of mine were easily replaced.

Sunflower and vegetable oils were swapped out for coconut and extra-virgin, when I discovered the former pair were by products of chemical refinement. Water from the tap tastes like the sewage it shares a pipe with and for a while now I had been purifying and ionizing my water, raising the PH level and actively helping me to heal and as one of the secrets to a long and healthy life was "surplus energy in a hydrated, alkaline environment," I had ironically become seriously addicted to the stuff.

I didn't drive, so didn't need to worry about spending large portions of my day sitting on top of a pile of batteries, destroying my body's electro-magnetic field. I had walked everywhere and back for all of my life up to this point and now was the proud owner of a new walking style and I planned to parade it up and down before it deserted me entirely.

My food now all came from local farmers, or should I say local farmer, as we were now sadly down to one in a ten-mile radius. Originally there were three producers I used to buy from, though two were now paid by the government NOT to farm. They had leased and then sold their land, which was now given over to rapeseed and assorted GMO crops, that were routinely sprayed with chemicals that killed every living thing in the field and eventually would do the same to the gullible saps the crop was fed to. Tobacco had been replaced with Cannabis and wine was waiting for its replacement as we spoke.

So, all of my short-cuts to short-term pleasure had been re-routed, apart from, as Dorian had brutally pointed out, the masturbation. As embarrassing of a subject as it may be, I found myself able to think about it without feeling as baseless and banal as I first imagined I would when explaining it. So here goes.

A stomach procedure earlier in the year had me bed-bound for some weeks, with instructions from the surgeon not to engage in any sexual activity (including masturbation) for the following eight weeks. Being a man, obviously I left it about eight hours before I decided to expel some energy and have a bit of a stroke. Sadly, however, things didn't go to plan. The muscles I had had repaired convulsed and tightened making the orgasm truly painful; so much so that I abandoned the climax halfway through and was hating myself well before the clean-up had started.

The next time I tried it, I started to feel anxious about the pain before it even started. As a result of this the ensuing orgasm produced fluid though no feeling.

The time after that produced feeling but no fluid and then produced neither of either. The last wank I ever had was abandoned before the "point of no return" as the self-loathing had kicked in almost immediately and it was with a mixture of triumph and defeat, of pride and shame, that I put myself away for the final time.

Some months later I would learn that the pulse I had learned to generate in my solar plexus, was much more powerful than any orgasm I had ever had, was stronger than any crack I had smoked, any ecstasy I had danced the night away to and any person I had ever loved, including Irene. It was the ultimate rush, the ultimate aphrodisiac, the ultimate high, so whenever I felt the urge to feel amazing immediately, that is where I went.

On the tube to Finsbury Park, I sent a quick text to Grace and apologized profusely for missing her yoga class that morning. When I say I apologized, what I really did was blame it entirely on her. I told her that meeting her and the wonderful night we had spent at the Diogenes Club afterwards had relaxed my mind and body so much so, that for once I hadn't needed Marijuana to sleep, had slept a solid eight hours without waking and when I did, was free of the aches and pains that normally accompany the first hours of my day.

As a rule at night, normally I don't fall asleep, what I do is pass out, so in the mornings I don't wake up, I come round and it usually takes me three coffees and two Vipes to smooth the creases out and generally for life to get going again with any purpose. I told her that I felt years younger and inches longer already and that to prove to her that I was committed to the program, I was only five minutes from the Buddhist Centre at that very moment, so if she could find a t-shirt and a pair of joggers in the lost and found box, then I would love to join her three o'clock meditation class, if there was any space.

I didn't need to dress it up so much, as she was neither angry nor happy with me in the slightest. She replied that she didn't mind, didn't take it personally and told me I must have had my reasons, and that as long as there wasn't any intention of hurting anybody when I made the decision not to come, then whatever I did instead was the right thing to do. I left it there and decided not to spoil things by telling her the real reason I was coming to the gym was entirely selfish. The class she was holding this afternoon was suitably titled "The Mindfulness of Breathing" and almost more than anything right now, that's what I needed to do. I say almost, as what I honestly and truly needed to do was to stop thinking. I needed to clear my mind, which was something that today for some reason, I couldn't do by myself.

I arrived at the Buddhist Centre and after donning the appropriate attire, which had been left for me at reception, I entered the small hall with my mat and blanket and walked quietly and respectfully to the back, purposefully avoiding any eye contact with Grace.

Sitting cross-legged was out of the question however; I wasn't feeling so supple, so I opted to kneel. I pulled my blanket around me and clasped my hands together just in time, as the singing bowl chimed its first.

After a quick body scan and clear instructions from Grace not to take any notice of external sounds, we were asked to hold a private party in our gardens and with each of us being the host, we were only allowed to invite three people. The first person we were asked to invite was someone that you saw every day but had no relation to you. We were asked to start up a conversation with them, to wish them well, to wish them happiness and good fortune. This was easy enough, though I instantly wished that I hadn't invited Mrs. Hudson. Firstly, she was one of the reasons for me coming here in the first place and secondly, I found that when face to face with her, away from Baker Street, I realized that we had nothing at all in common and had run out of things to talk about almost immediately.

The second chime came on the fifteen-minute mark, and we were asked to invite and introduce somebody we love to the party. Another quarter of an hour later, we were asked to finally invite and introduce somebody that we hate, which, if everyone got along, would carry us through to the forty-five-minute mark and then we would probably have some chit chat to the final bell. After spending too long scrabbling around trying to come up with somebody I loved and then again spending too much time trying to choose from the people I hated, I gave Mrs. Hudson a glass of prosecco and then hid behind the curtain for the last half hour and watched her walk around the garden alone, talking to herself. Apart from stifling a laugh due to the absurdity of the situation, in time I started to drift off where I knelt. In the distance, I heard Grace begin to talk, though as per her instructions, I didn't let the sound of her voice intrude on my thoughts. My mind had become beautifully clear. I recognized the sound, accepted it for what it was, let it come towards me and just let it pass by. It was something about life-force energy and the importance of not forcing it. The awakening, she said, would come when we knew where we were in the world and had accepted all things.

Both of my legs had fallen fast asleep, and my body was about to follow, when a voice right beside me said.

"Do you know where you are in the world, Sherlock?"

I awoke to the unsettling vision of Mycroft sneering down at me like Rigsby from Rising Damp. The class had been dismissed, and I was knelt alone at the back of the hall. I had to sit for a second and take his scorn, as walking, for the moment was completely out of the question. I stretched my legs out in front of me and started to fold the blanket and allow them to regain their strength.

"Not particularly," I said, "Like most people, my pendulum seems to swing between overstating my importance in the universe and accepting my soul-crushing insignificance in it. My default setting, however, is to remain constantly aware of my limited relevance. Does that answer your question? What are you doing here?"

Mycroft turned on his heel and strode away. "Let's get a cup of tea," he said.

As I showered, Mycroft wandered about the changing room with his tea. The smile and contented sigh from him told me that the Buddhist Centre Green Cafe luckily stocked Chinese tea, for that is the only tea he drank and though it was my preferred tea of choice now that coffee had to go, I obviously wouldn't be choosing the same, just out of stubborn-faced pride. As usual my brother declined the opportunity to say something nice.

"Wouldn't know the difference between a Lhasa Apso and a Lapsang Souchong. I've never really bought in to this hippy way of life, as you know, Sherlock; most of it is just pure laziness. It's a lifestyle that purports to be a refuge for artists, musicians, poets and dreamers. The bohemian bourgeoisie, if you will. In reality, it's a collection of pot heads, criminals, lost souls, fake healers and trustafarians. Smoked salmon socialism

I call it. I do believe you when you say that you don't know where you are in the world Sherlock.... but do you know...?"

I tried to think of his voice as a car outside, I recognized it as an external sound, acknowledged it, noticed it getting closer and just as I was about to let it pass by, it stopped suddenly right in front of me. I wiped the soap from my face, which was inches from my brother's, staring at me over the cubicle door. He was suddenly serious.

"Where in the world Dorian is?" he said.

I was ready for him and didn't flinch. "Who the hell is Dorian?" I asked.

Mycroft drew his lips into a weak smile, turned and strode out of the changing room.

"I'll be in the cafe," he said.

When I had showered and changed, I got myself a Jasmine tea and joined Mycroft, who was sitting on a sofa with one arm stretched over the back, like he owned the place. I sat on the sofa opposite, but before I could question him any further on his unexpected and unwelcome appearance here, he apologized.

"Sorry for the intrusion," he said. "In my professional experience, naked men tend not to lie."

I ignored him and looked about for any sign of Grace. I winced. "So why do I get the feeling that you still don't believe me?"

He continued. "Your missing politician and the body in the drain. You have figured out that the same person is responsible for both, I take it."

I nodded. "Almost immediately."

Mycroft sipped thoughtfully on his tea. "I guessed as much. Which is why I think that he has been in touch. He hasn't tried to contact you?"

I really didn't have the time to play twenty questions with

him. Impatiently I looked around again for Grace. Not only would she save me from the torture of talking to my brother, but the child in me wanted her to see I was drinking green tea before I finished it. I tried not to let him get to me and undo all the good personal work I had put in this morning. He always had the ability to wind me up, but I was determined not to let it happen here.

"No, he hasn't," I replied. "And why are you so interested? And how do you know his name?"

Mycroft took his phone from his jacket and showed me a photo on it. I was none the wiser.

"Is that him?" I asked.

Mycroft eyed me suspiciously but carried on. "Montague Frobisher," he said. "A banker. Not the teller at your high street branch though and forget about banks in the City, the Central Bank and the IMF. I take it you have heard of the Bank of International Settlements?"

I had heard, but only that. I nodded. "More powerful than the Vatican and the Club of Rome...and twice as secretive."

Mycroft smiled and nodded. "Exactly right," he agreed. "The police can't touch them, the military can't touch them, they can buy and sell gold privately. Well, Mr. Frobisher is the name of your pile of bones. He was at the Diogenes two nights ago."

Mycroft pulled up another photo on his phone and showed it to me. "With him. Have you ever seen him before?"

The image was a still taken from the entrance to the Diogenes. A few people were in the shot but, in front and center, without a shadow of doubt, was Dorian. I was bored. Where was Grace?

"No, Mycroft. How could I have possibly seen him? That's Dorian is it? Well, we were both at the Diogenes two nights ago...was he there? It's your club. You should know."

"They were in a private room. Obviously, there are no cameras in there, we just managed to get a few of these shots when they were leaving. Mr. Frobisher left with one of the waitresses, though she assures me, if it is a she that there was a pre-arranged sexual transaction in the alleyway and then she went home. Thing is, at the same time that he was leaving with her, his remains were also being fished out of the drain. See the problem? All the members of that party are accounted for, except this guy. None of them had ever met him before and nobody knows where he went. All they know is, his name is Dorian and he was making a private donation."

Mycroft leaned forward and clasped his hands together. He was deadly serious again.

"Are you quite sure he hasn't been in touch?"

I looked around once more for Grace and gulped the rest of my tea. "No, he hasn't, but if he does..."

"If he does, you will still lie to my face and say he hasn't, because even though I think I know you better than anyone, you also know me better than anyone and we cancel each other out. We believe that this Dorian has special abilities and that is why I'm so interested. We need to work together on this one, Sherlock...there's more at stake than you can possibly imagine."

"Oh, don't be so dramatic!" I said.

All of a sudden, the word "Chinese" popped into my head and in two shakes of a lamb's tail, I had launched myself over the back of the sofa and straight out of the front door.

I knew full well that Mycroft would hunt down and interrogate Grace, but I figured for her having too much in her locker to answer any of his questions. I jumped on the tube to Baker Street and was back in the flat, replete with food within the hour, which we ate around the kitchen table in complete silence and though the reasons for Dr Watson's and Mrs. Hudson's silence were unknown to me, my own reasons were many and varied. My memory was my main concern. All the way home I had given myself little exercises to do, games I normally play to keep my mind sharp, and I had failed each one as if for fun. Right now, I was trying to figure out why. I suspect that a part of Dr. Watson's silence was pretty much for the same reason as mine, though I guessed that my learned friend was too polite and too hungry to say anything, though no doubt he would soon enough. I glanced at him through the top of my head. His hunger had kept him quiet so far, but I knew that once his appetite had been slaked, he would be all over me.

How did I know this? Because he had just wolfed down a plate of food he clearly didn't ask for and the minute he was to finish, then we would play the game again of how my mind was failing me and I should go and see a professional and how he and Mrs. Hudson were worried about me. Mrs. Hudson said she was worried about me, but she reserved a peculiar line of abuse for me that made me question her concern, though I admit that this particular torrent was entirely my own fault. I was still bent out of shape over her comments about my body and today was the first time I had found time to address the situation. I shouldn't have bothered. "Got a comment at the gym today," I said.

There wasn't a sound, save for the clink of cutlery... nobody said a word, but they were obviously dying to know. I decided to push the point along but cue the absolutist. "Thought it was a Buddhist Centre you went to," he muttered around his chopsticks. I ignored him and continued.

"Said I had the body of a dancer," I announced triumphantly.

Mrs. Hudson snorted into her soup. "Sod off, Sherlock, I've seen you dance. Remember last Halloween, when you went to that party as Jack the Stripper. We thought there was something wrong with you, didn't we, Dr. Watson? We thought that you were allergic to music."

Dr. Watson stifled an embarrassed laugh, and Mrs. Hudson shook her silly little head when she giggled, and they had a right little old laugh at my expense. I wasn't offended, or hurt, or ashamed, or anything...much...at all...the bastards. I stared at them both in amazement but eventually saw the funny side of it and laughed along with them. I didn't suddenly see their point of view but had laughed at the image I had of the party in question, of me standing in Trafalgar Square in a top hat and cloak, with a cane, fishnets and high heels, trying to get a taxi at three in the morning. Whatever the cause for my climb down, it was ruined as usual by Dr. Watson driving a horse and cart right through the conversation and the mood. He just couldn't help himself.

"Lovely this, Sherlock. Not at all what I asked for, but very nice. One thing too hard to remember, was it?"

I stared at him as I chewed. "You're lucky you got anything," I said. "I'm having some problems recalling certain things. I'm looking into it," I reassured him.

Mrs. Hudson chewed thoughtfully. Her eyebrows narrowed over her fork. "I wouldn't like to try finding anything in your head, Sherlock," she said. "It'd be like looking for a noodle in a nutsack."

Dr. Watson laughed heartily at this and banged his hand on the table. "Brilliant, Mrs. Hudson...I think you'll find the phrase is, looking for a needle in a hayst..."

"I know perfectly well what the phrase is, Dr. Watson," she interrupted, "have you ever seen the inside of a nutsack?"

The good doctor's mouth dropped open. He stared at Mrs. Hudson and then he turned to me, as if for support, but he wasn't going to get any.

"She's absolutely right!" I announced, continuing to eat

around my words. "It would be a damn sight more difficult to spot. To date, I have tried to find ten needles in ten different haystacks and each time I have found the needle in under five minutes. Flatten the bale and spread the hay out across the floor, then take a large magnet and drag it over the surface. Needle jumps out. Problem solved. I think trying to locate a noodle in a nutsack would be virtually impossible."

Dr. Watson looked glum. He absent-mindedly pushed his food around his plate...talk of testicles had evidently ruined his appetite. Mrs. Hudson tried to lighten the mood by changing the subject. "They are very good at balancing flavors the Chinese, aren't they? Japanese too."

Dr. Watson took the way out by jumping straight in, suddenly the world's leading authority on the senses. "Umami, Mrs. Hudson," he exclaimed. "It's like a sixth sense, where all the flavors come together, bitter, sweet, salty, sour, savory...the Spanish call it "la lingua" ...like having a G-spot on the tongue...if you'll pardon my vulgarity."

No such apology was needed, however. Mrs. Hudson's face lit up. Oh, I know exactly the thing, Dr. Watson," she remarked. "It reminds me of that famous seventies' film, ooh, it's a classic.... girl had something wrong with her throat... I can see her now, long brown hair, sitting on a bed, stuff coming out of her mouth...Linda, Linda, Linda something..."

A triumphant look came over the good doctor, he smiled at me, just as he did when he beat me to the name of the German chef. "Aah...Linda Blair...Exorcist!" he announced proudly.

"Deepthroat!" shouted Mrs. Hudson, "that's the one."

Dr Watson spat his food straight across the table, then sat for a few uncomfortable seconds with his bulging eyes turned on my housekeeper, as he tried to negotiate a noodle back up his nose, from where it dangled.

Mrs. Hudson wasn't fazed. "I only saw the first five

minutes," she said. "Linda Lovelace. Poor girl had a (and here she mouthed the word) clit-o-ris in the back of her throat."

"Mrs. Hudson!" Dr. Watson spluttered finally.

I laughed at them both heartily, wiped my plate and pushed it to the center of the table. "I thoroughly enjoyed that, Mrs. Hudson," I remarked, "it was fantastic...where did you learn to cook like that?"

Mrs. Hudson and Dr. Watson gave each other knowing looks. He raised his eyebrows and she giggled. "Oh, it's just a few things I threw together, Sherlock," she said. Dr. Watson began to have some kind of seizure. He coughed and spluttered into his handkerchief, his eyes darting manically from myself to Mrs. Hudson. He swallowed the food in his mouth and stared at us both in utter disbelief. Finally, he spoke.

"You couldn't make it up," he offered, still glancing at us both; "Finding Dorian and Finding Dory... I can't fucking take any more," he said.

"Language at the table, thank you," scolded Mrs. Hudson.

Dr. Watson got to his feet in a huff, put his plate in the sink and started to hastily get his things together. I understood his frustration. It was bad enough trying to cope with the deterioration of Mrs. Hudson; he was hardly going to be overjoyed that I had joined her on that particular slope. I didn't like to see him leaving in a bad mood though.

"Where are you going," I asked.

The poor doctor looked and sounded completely worn out by it all.

"I don't know," he replied. "I think I'm going to go and quietly shoot myself in the face. Home, Sherlock, I'm going home. I'll be here tomorrow first thing to give you your jab."

"You bloody won't, you know," I spluttered. "I'm having a day off. I have something I have to do tomorrow. Make it the day after."

Dr. Watson put on his hat and raincoat and looked at me

with a kind of sadness, but that feeling and situation had passed me by and my head was full of magic. Apart from days of the week, what can you think of that there are seven of?"

Mrs. Hudson was still picking at her food; she looked sad and confused. "Brides and brothers," she muttered.

The doctor had not yet admitted defeat. and he rounded on me for another attempt.

"Stop putting it off, Sherlock. I'll be here about eleven. Dwarves."

I wasn't listening to him. "What?"

"Seven dwarves," he said.

"I doubt it, but thanks," I replied. "I'm out early in the morning and then I'm busy all day, so not tomorrow. Leave it till the day after, please." I filled my Vipe and sat in silence in my armchair, miles away. The doctor wasn't prepared to leave without some kind of promise from me. He prodded again.

"I know that you have a phobia about needles now, Sherlock, and that's perfectly understandable...in and out...you won't even know it's happened."

I ignored him. He stood in the doorway, then taking his cue from Mrs. Hudson, he quietly left the apartment. I sat in silence, puffed on my Vipe and stared into space. In time I detected movement behind me. I looked to see Mrs. Hudson still sitting at the dining table. She had her back turned to me and her shoulders shook in silence. Was she crying? "Mrs. Hudson!" I exclaimed jumping to my feet. I put away my Vipe went to her and crouched in front of her. Tears were streaming down her face without a sound. She looked heartbroken, I wonder what on Earth was wrong. I thought better of wiping her eyes but handed her a tissue.

"Come on, Mrs. Hudson," I said, "you're going to spoil your makeup."

She looked down at me, her face screwed up and she shook her head."

I was shocked at how upset she was. I looked into her eyes. "Mrs. Hudson," I said, "whatever is the matter?"

She twisted the handkerchief through her fingers and started to sob again. "Oh, Sherlock!" she said. "I don't even have a wok."

CHAPTER NINE

ESCAPE TO THE SHITHOLE

The law of vibration states that nothing rests and out of respect for this law, that night I didn't either, but instead fidgeted like a sparrow by the window until the day was about to break, then I set off before the city awoke. The squalid Victorian streets of London can still be found, should you have a mind to seek them out and that morning seek them out I did. Two hundred years ago, having a mind to do so was wholly unnecessary, as was indeed the need to seek them out, as the acrid stench from the River Thames would restore any partially functional nose to full working order in no time and would guide a man with no mind and no senses through watering eyes without incident, to his dank and rancid destination. Likewise, nowadays a mind would again be considered a luxury, as independent thought and free enquiry were now frowned upon, though ironically without Google Maps I wouldn't have found this place at all.

I stood and looked towards the river, down a street that the march of time had left standing. A small puddle of houses was slung to one side of a street which formed part of a labyrinthine network of slum terracing, that at one time incorporated the infamous Frying Pan Alley and it was towards this pile of bricks, on slimy broken Yorkstone flags that I pointed my feet and skidded and slid towards the front door of my intended destination. I didn't knock too hard, for fear of putting the door through, but loud enough and long enough to bring the proprietor scurrying down behind it. I was greeted by a short, wiry old chap, who turned on his heel and without a word, bounded expertly up the rickety staircase in front of me like a leopard. There was a crooked man, who owned a crooked flat, I climbed the crooked staircase, took off my crooked hat, he offered crooked terms, for a crooked monthly lease, to give my crooked mind, a bit of bloody peace. I stood next to him and looked from the filthy windows down on to the sinister scene below. The old man was no estate agent, and he obviously didn't feel the need to struggle for superlatives but instead chose to confront any awkwardness head-on with a self-deprecating humor. He jangled the keys in his pocket.

"Horrible, isn't it" he said.

It wasn't a question. I couldn't have agreed more. It was thoroughly miserable. I beamed at him and removed a wad of notes from my wallet. "Yes," I agreed. "It's perfect." The muddy banks slipped into the dismal water, which ran rank from East to West not yards from my front door. It was dark and depressing and it hurt one's heart to look at, but for me it was without equal. One could almost say that as a view, it was peerless.

I paid the man a month up front and another month to keep my tenancy an absolute secret and when he had left I walked the rooms to get a feel for the place. The layout was essentially a kitchen, a living room, a bathroom and a bedroom, though it took the term "unfurnished" to a new level, in so much as the carpets had all been lifted and taken away and the wallpaper had peeled itself from the walls and disappeared. The kitchen had a cooker, a fridge and nothing else, the bedroom had a bed in a room and nothing else and was tiny. The bathroom had no bath whatsoever and only qualified as a room because it had a door. There was a partially working toilet and a foul-smelling liquid rust that filled the cistern and spluttered from the taps. The room itself was so tiny, I would have to go outside to change my mind. In the living room, there was a dark stain in the middle of the floor. "From what?" I wondered as I stared down at it. This house and this room especially had no doubt seen its fair share of pain and misery.

For the past couple of centuries this house had probably been home to several families at once. Surely somebody had died in here...maybe right there. The ragged souls who had inhabited these dwellings in days gone by had died from consumption, from toothache, from lack of care and basic provisions, the bare essentials to stay alive, but mostly they died from disease. Some poor wretch had probably died right there on the floor of the living room and no doubt lay there for days, with their body fermenting in its own footprint and the acids etching the owner's soul into the floorboards. But no more suffering, no more deprivation, no more hardship...at one time a sticky shadow trapped forever between floors and now just a forgotten stain. The ceilings were high, so the walls were vast and ready to be written on. In order to solve this puzzle, I needed to go right back to basics, no google, no wiki, no Bing, no TikTok, in fact no electronic help of any kind... just me and a pen, a blank wall and my mind...if indeed I still had one.

I grabbed my bag and removed the headset from it, seated myself at the only armchair and turned the thing on. As expected, the circle and star insignia appeared, started to spin, then slowly exploded and started to turn on their axes. All of a sudden, a message appeared on the screen...it said, "Go on, have a guess."

I removed the headset and took a sketch pad from my bag. I then tore off each page and Blu-Tacked side by side over the whole expanse of the wall. I then took my pen and wrote the numbers one to seven down the length of it. I put the headset back on, but on the screen nothing had changed. I removed the headset and stood by the window staring out.

"Seven.....seven what?"

I threw the headset back into my bag, closed the window, donned my hat and coat and left the flat.

When I returned to Baker Street, Mrs. Hudson was in the process of leaving for the day. I stood there soaked and watched her scurry about for a few seconds.

"You're breakfast is in the oven, Sherlock," she announced. "There are things in the freezer for your dinner tonight, so you'll have to take something out. Don't forget I'm going out again with the girls tonight. I'm going to see that Irish singer I like. And what have I told you about taking your wet clothes off at the door?" I looked down at the small puddles that were forming at my feet.

"Dr. Watson doesn't take off his wet clothes, and you don't get on his case about it," I responded.

"Two wrongs don't make a right, Sherlock," she said.

I stepped back over towards the door and did as I was instructed. "But three lefts do!" I said. This stopped the good lady in her tracks. She stopped and stared at me.

"Three lefts? What on Earth are you talking about, Sherlock?"

"Two wrongs don't make a right, but three lefts do."

I watched her eyes, as she attempted to perform the necessary maneuver in her head, but I could see that she had reversed out of her parking space in the alleyway behind the flat, realized she had started going off the wrong way and stalled the car. I couldn't watch any more. I opened the oven and retrieved my breakfast, while rummaging through my files for Irish singers. I gave up almost immediately. "What Irish singer?" I asked.

Mrs. Hudson thought for a moment. "That girl with the telephone on her head," she replied... "Lady O'Gaga."

I looked at her briefly, thought of correcting her, but found that I couldn't muster the enthusiasm. "Okay, no problem," I said.

At this, Mrs. Hudson smiled and continued her exit routine, singing as she went.

"All we hear is, Lady O'Gaga...Lady O'Googoo.... someone still loves you." Mrs. Hudson's capacity to murder a song was universally recognized, her fading memory notwithstanding. In terms of her prowess, she had such a vast repertoire that I labelled her a serial killer of songs, though she was a classically trained pianist and had been in a girl band back in the eighties, the name escapes me now. The Ditsy Chicks... The Bundy Sisters perhaps."

After breakfast, I filled my Vipe and settled into my chair. Mrs. Hudson got her things together and left me and the day to ourselves, which passed in a confusion of snacks and splintered dreams. I dreamed of temples and pyramids, of fractions and fractals, of Gods and dragons and spinning spheres and even though I had my eyes closed for the best part of the day, I awoke exhausted to find that Mrs. Hudson had been back, covered me in my chair and disappeared again, leaving me alone to twist and turn through the night. Life got going again the next morning, when Mrs. Hudson barreled through the flat with her daily intake of provisions. Or most of them.

"I got everything you asked me to," she informed me. "Well, almost everything. I got the PH tester and the acids. I didn't get any gold though. That was a joke, right?"

My head shot from under the duvet; to find out I was lying on the floor. I looked around.

"That was the one thing I really needed," I said. I got to my feet and sat in my armchair.

"Haven't you got any old rings or chains you don't wear?",

Mrs. Hudson stopped and looked at me quizzically. "I might have," she said. "I take it I won't be getting them back. Why, what is it you want it for?"

I felt suddenly energized when I remembered what I had to do. I sprung to my feet. "I am going to melt them it down and then turn it into a white powder."

Mrs. Hudsons face fell. "Oh, Sherlock, you can't just leave it alone, can you?" she scolded.

I laughed, "Oh it's nothing like that, Mrs. Hudson. Don't worry." I went over to her and kissed the top of her head, but the woman was not for turning. She shrugged me off and carried on with her duties. "Well, whatever it is you're planning, you're not doing it here," she remarked. "I have to put my foot down, Sherlock. No more fires, no more explosions, no more meltdowns. My heart is worse than my memory and it can't take it anymore."

I completely understood Mrs. Hudson's concerns; exactly how this house of hers was still standing I probably wouldn't live long enough to comprehend. I started to gather the bottles together and started to fit them into my backpack.

"I know," I relented. "I won't be doing it here. I'll be away for a few days."

An alarm went off in my head, and I started to pick up the pace. I had to get out of here quickly. Mrs. Hudson looked at me with complete surprise. "Why, where are you going?" she said.

I danced into my shoes and grabbed the nearest coat to hand, checked my bag, zipped it up and threw it over my shoulder. "Get the gold," I said.

Mrs. Hudson disappeared and returned with a small

handful of twisted chains and rings, which I fairly snatched from her hand and stuffed them deep into the pocket of my overcoat. She still looked concerned. "So where are you going to be?" she asked. I gave Mrs. Hudson a quick hug and another kiss on top of her head. "Mrs. Hudson, don't worry, I won't be far. I'll ask Dr. Watson to stay with you for a couple of days."

I was about to open the door, when the door opened and there stood Dr. Watson like an angel of death. He stood, stock still and a cunning smile crept over his face. Sometimes I fucking hated him.

"Going somewhere, Holmes?" He laughed. "I thought you might try and get out of it, so I came a bit earlier."

I panicked and decided to try to bluff my way out of it. "Sorry, can't stop, Watson," I blurted out, trying to edge past him in the doorway. Dr. Watson pushed me back into the room, closed the door and locked it behind him with the key. He then dumped his bags on the table and strolled over to the fridge. He removed the vaccine from the door, a syringe from his bag and addressed me again.

"I told you I would be giving you your jab today. Roll your sleeve up!"

I ignored the doctor and started to rummage through a drawer in the sideboard for the spare key to the front door. I was starting to lose my temper with him.

"Dr. Watson, I appreciate that you have my best interests at heart, but you really have to stop going on about it. You're no more still a doctor than you are still a soldier. I don't do needles anymore and you more than anyone should have a bit more understanding...I'm still a high-functioning sociopath with..."

At this point Dr. Watson exploded. "No, you're not!" he screamed. "You have severe, recurrent and chronic major depression with psychotic features."

"W..." I began.

"I haven't finished! And you have an adjustment disorder with depression and anxiety, with paranoid schizophrenic and borderline personality traits. This isn't about you, Sherlock. It's about protecting vulnerable people from you."

I was numb. I was shocked and saddened by this sudden explosion from Dr. Watson. I stood and stared at him and slowly started to roll up my sleeve. I relented not because for over a week I had promised both him and Mrs. Hudson that I would follow government advice, or protocol, or mandate, or orders, or whatever they were now. Nor did I back down because of the withering though precise description of my current mental condition. I gave in to him for the very simple reason, that I had an amazing day planned, that included neither of those two, nor anybody else. I only wanted one thing right then at that particular moment, and that was to get the fuck out of there. I held my arm out as Dr. Watson prepared the syringe. I also held his gaze and tried to think of something else, but that was much easier said than done. I somehow remembered that every cell in the human body generates 0.07 Millivolts of electricity and tried to send a pulse out to calm my nerves, but they were screaming in protest and impossible to be calm. Dr. Watson didn't know enough about the cause he was fighting for to be forcing this situation on me. Forever one to jump to the government's defense, virtue signaling had become an annoying trait of his and though largely I was able to ignore it, this concerned me greatly as it wasn't just my health at stake here, but possibly my very life.

I wanted to pull my arm away, but I wanted to leave my apartment much more. I guessed that there would be seven deaths of prominent figures, maybe over a seven-day period. I also noticed that Dr. Watson had seven buttons on his shirt and seven eye holes in his shoes.

His hand shook terribly, as he waved the syringe in the

direction of my arm. I held his wrist to steady it and guided the needle to a vein I had not seen for years. A sadness suddenly overtook me. I gazed into my good friend's eyes, not trying to hide the single tear that escaped down my face and as he fired the dubious payload into my bloodstream, I knew that this was much more than a jab and that something between us, maybe the very thing that held us together, was broken and gone for good. Mrs. Hudson was also in tears, but Dr. Watson held on to his stoic medical bearing to the end.

"I'm sorry, Sherlock. It's for your own good," he said.

I ignored him and rolled my sleeve back up in silence. Clearly it wasn't for my good, it was for his own and he knew it. Without another word, I threw on my coat, grabbed my bag and left the apartment.

On my way to the shithole, I learned from Dr. Watson that the priest who's awful death I had witnessed had a name and a parish in central London. and in that parish was a church, inside which his charred remains were placed on gruesome display. The text I had received was perfunctory and businesslike. The doctor had some groveling to do, and I had no intention of letting him off the hook just yet. Hopefully he would feel guilty enough to leave me alone for the few days I needed. What I did need, however, was Grace's help.

I arrived at the shithole and within half an hour she appeared in the street, staring up at my window. I threw the window open and with a finger on my lips, beckoned her to the front door. I hurtled down the stairs and swung open the front door.

"Quick, quick, inside," I said. "Did anyone follow you?"

Grace was soaking wet and looking and smelling wonderful as usual.

"Why would anyone follow me?" she asked in amusement. "Sherlock, what is going on?"

I grabbed her by her bag and fairly dragged her into the hallway and booted her up the stairs.

"Up, up, up, quick!"

After unceremoniously shoving her into the flat, she stopped and gazed open-mouthed at the state of the place. In the hour or so that I had been there, I had added a map of the world and a few lists I thought might be pertinent to the investigation. Grace spun slowly on her heel and took it all in. She took a tissue from her coat pocket, held it to her nose and gagged into her hand. "Sherlock, what is that awful smell?"

I'd completely forgotten I had Mrs. Hudson's jewelry cooking away on the stove. I closed the kitchen door and threw the living room window open. "Tea?" I asked. Grace shook her head...quite right too, as I had no teabags, sugar or milk and if I had such ingredients, I still didn't have a kettle. If I'd have had a kettle, then I would have no cups or space on the stove, nor any electricity or running water. I might as well have asked her if she wanted a cup of the sperm of Horus, also known as the Elixir of Life, Philosopher's Stone or whatever, as right now, of the two, the latter would be infinitely more attainable, as I was in the process of making some.

I stood beaming at her, as she continued to scan the walls around us. She finally spoke. "No, thank you," she said. "Sherlock, what is going on? What have you got yourself in to? And why is everybody looking for you?"

I motioned her to the only sittable chair. "Alright, bloody hell, Jeremy Paxman." I laughed. "Sit down and I'll tell you."

Grace perched on the end of the chair, folded her hands on her lap and smiled at me.

"I'm listening," she said.

I positioned myself cross-legged on the floor in front of her, steepled my fingers under my chin and began.

"What I am about to tell you, might seem a little far-fetched, but please, I implore you to bear with me. You are the only person I know who will understand it and you are definitely the only person who can help me solve it." I reached out and clasped her hands. "Will you help me?" "I'll try," she replied.

I jumped to my feet and started to stride about the room. "Excellent, that's a good start. Right, I am involved in a case, a murder case. Two so far and soon to be three. All high profile victims...a banker, probably a politician...."

Suddenly Grace's phone received a message. I stared at her as she read it. I was silently livid. "And a priest by any chance?" I asked without wanting to know. Grace looked up at me and knew instantly why I was annoyed. She looked sheepish though a bit surprised and held her phone out towards me. Her message was from Dr. Watson...it said:

"If you hear from Sherlock, please ask him to call me. Father O'Driscoll found burned to death on his altar. St Johns Church in Whitechapel. Mycroft has taken the body.

Watson."

I waved the message away. "I thought that would happen. It doesn't matter. I have all the details. And turn your bloody phone off," I snapped, "the whole point of being here is being anonymous."

Grace stared back at me, as she turned her phone off. "How did you know about the priest?" she asked.

I went to my backpack and retrieved the headset from it. I stopped and looked at her. "Because I watched it happen through this," I said. "I saw him kill the priest through this. He sends me messages through this and the odd live event. There's a giant puzzle I have to solve...no googling! But I can't send messages and it apparently doesn't work on anyone else." To prove my point, I slipped it over Grace's head and switched it on. "See anything?" Grace shook her head and took it off. "No. Nothing."

I took a sharpie from my bag, went over the largest of the blank walls of the flat and slipped the headset on again. To the best of my ability, I started to draw on the wall what I was seeing on the screen.

"Okay, what I have here," I began, "are circles...maybe fifty of them, a few different sizes...and triangles, all isosceles... seven of them...and everything is spinning around, on its own axis and in its own orbit."

I discarded the headset and drew what I could from what memory I had left and as I did, I gave Grace a running commentary. "Okay, originally what I was seeing was an emblem, a motif...black and gold. My opponent in this seems to be a chap called Dorian, who represents something called The Council of Seven. So, I'm guessing that the puzzle is all based around the number seven. What I see is an exploded image of the same thing and through a series of tests and clues and bodies, I guess the challenge is to put the motif back together and in doing so, the world back to rights. I have to solve it or find Dorian and stop him before he kills seven people. Then hopefully I can prevent the slaughter that would happen if I don't solve it.

"The slaughter of who?" asked Grace, coming up beside me.

I stopped scribbling on the wall and turned to face her, tears of pride and sadness pricking my eyes. I smiled and looked back at the wall.

"Of everyone on Earth," I said.

Grace gave me a look of disbelief. I felt suddenly energized and started to pick up the pace. I started to draw quickly.

"So, as I say," I announced. "About fifty circles, I can't remember for sure and now they are all spinning around and you can't see them. There was a seven-pointed star in the center, that I do know. Then I think there were seven groups of seven that I have to figure out and somehow fit them in the puzzle. There were a couple of bigger circles in sections, but as I say I really can't remember. All the circles and triangles turned together, like the mechanism of a watch or a clock. So if we start on lists of seven, I have ruled out brides and brothers, colors of the rainbow and dwarves. I seem to be having trouble with my memory."

This was all too sudden and too quick for Grace, I'm not sure I was making much sense to her right now. She tried to take me by the arm. "Sherlock, slow down," she said.

"Sherlock, sit down for a second...Sherlock...sit down... Sherlock!"

I stopped and stared at her. She was right, this must have been impossible to grasp.

"What do you mean, everyone on Earth?" she asked. "Who is this person?"

I couldn't slow down. I looked back at the wall. "I'm not really sure it is a who in the conventional sense. He takes the form of a man but that's where it stops. He can travel vast distances in a heartbeat. He disappears here and re-appears over there; I have footage of him doing it. He is, I believe, an inter-dimensional entity, either from our past or from our future...and if I've got this right, then seven people are going to die, and I have to get to him before he gets to them.

Grace was now slowly starting to grasp the magnitude of the situation. She looked crestfallen. "And if you don't?" she asked.

"I'm afraid that this planet has had enough of us, my dear Grace, and this man, being, entity or whatever he is, has been sent to wipe us all out."

"Do you think you can stop him."

"If I can find out how he is moving around, maybe."

"Any ideas?"

I was already on the move. I moved to the kitchen and bid Grace follow me. I threw open the window, as Grace went for her tissue again. She stared at the assortment of flasks and test tubes set up on the kitchen table. On the stove top, a pan boiled away furiously. I smiled at her and despite the toxicity of the air around us, I took a deep breath. "Please just for a second, spare me a small slice of your imagination," I said. "Back in the eighties, a dirt farmer from Texas, David Hudson...no relation...well he was hired as a troubleshooter to go from mine to mine, giving advice on how to make the most profit from your mine. Golden Ramsay, if you will. He also mined his own gold and he was successful, until he started pulling out a strange substance that appeared wherever the gold was, that he couldn't separate from the gold and was causing him to lose money. He put the substance through a spectrograph, but apart from a small amount of nickel and iron, the substance wouldn't read. You might say that's impossible; it has to be something...and you'd be right. So, he sent the sample to Moscow and discovered what the problem was. When they heated it up, as expected, the elements would read, as they reached their burn temperature. At 45 tin would read, then nickel, then iron.... then nothing! But instead of stopping there, they continued to heat it...and after a hundred seconds, something began to happen. Iridium started to read...then Osmium, then Rhodium, then Palladium, Platinum and Ruthenium....all the heavy platinum metals began to read." I finally paused and looked at Grace. She looked like she was about to cry.

"You have completely lost me, Sherlock. I have absolutely no idea what you are talking about."

I completely understood her concern, but I was excited and gathering speed. She would get it soon enough.

"Well, here's the good bit. The sample was weighed, exposed to an inert gas, heated, then weighed again....and was only five ninths of its original weight. Cool the sample down, the substance came back. Isolate the substance, heat it up, it disappears, wave something over the tray, nothing there, it's gone...cool it down, it's back. If your brain isn't suitably fried already, check this out.... when this substance was heated up in the tray and it disappeared, it weighed less than the tray itself weighed, with nothing on it.

It was there, then it wasn't. The question is...where did it go?

Grace sat on the chair, bamboozled. "This Dorian said that ultimately the answers were to be found within," I continued, "so I'm guessing Chakras...seven of them. But I can't remember what they are."

Grace laughed. "How can you not remember?" she asked. "I only sent them to you a couple of days ago."

"I have them recorded under their Indian names," I replied tapping my temple, "but they are locked away."

Grace took the marker from me and started to write them on the wall. Root-Red, Sacrum-Orange, Solar-Plexus-Yellow, Heart-Green, Throat-Blue, Third Eye-Indigo and Crown-Violet.

She handed me the marker back. "Look familiar?" she asked.

I stared at them. "Nope!" I said.

All of a sudden a "whoosh" sound came from my bag. I exchanged brief glances with Grace and made a dive for it. I removed the headset and put it on. I couldn't stay inside of my skin. On the screen part of the puzzle started to come back together. I felt for the wall and drew what I was seeing.

"We were right," I exclaimed. "It's Chakras! It works. Okay game on. We have a seven-pointed star in the center. The rest is still floating around."

I took the headset off and beamed at Grace. "My Dear Grace," I said, "the game is very much afoot."

Grace was less impressed. "You still haven't told me how he is disappearing and travelling through time," she said.

I moved quickly back into the kitchen. Grace followed.

"The mysterious substance that I was just telling you about, is made from the platinum-based metals in monatomic form, reduced and composed of single atoms, that don't cluster to form a metal. It's just a white powder. Like this it can be hydrated to form a kind of mucus, which when taken into the body, generates a flux-flow, like a superconductor and it moves around the body, repairing dead cells, without resistance...so it's pure energy...this is the secret the Egyptians had for a long life, the white powder gold, the tears of Horus, the elixir of life, the Philosopher's Stone, call it what you want. It also works with silver and gold, which through a complicated chemical process, which I am conducting here, can be reduced to a single atom...a white powder. This is one of the ancient secrets that have been hidden from humanity...and this afternoon, we are going to make some."

Grace stared at me sadly. I guessed that she didn't believe me.

"I take it you are a creationist," I said.

She took another look at the wall. "Yes, I am, but it isn't that. I believe what Dorian is saying is that the answer is found in each of us. The Holy spirit lives in us all, Sherlock... and yes, I do believe in God."

"Which one?" I asked.

"What do you mean?"

"Shiva? Apollo? Ganesh? Tuw? The word in the Bible is Elohim...it means Gods...it's plural. So, we're talking about multiple Gods. As you know, my mind runs on facts, on logic, data, evidence, science and to some extent reason. But let's just say that there is something inside us all, something that can be seen, can be measured, can be felt. What do you think that thing could be?"

Grace looked at me with incredulity. "Oh, you're talking about life-force energy. That's not meant to be taken literally."

I laughed. "I beg to differ," I said, "but we're getting somewhere. What we are talking about is Prana, or Xi. or Chi, or Ether as the Greeks called it. But I'm not looking for a provocative subtext here. I mean to say that a real substance, a flowing, life-giving plasma, that takes care of the body, that repairs it and keeps it alive. An etheric binder." I stared into the near distance and then went to stand by the window and looked into the darkening sky. "We get to move into the next dimension, Grace, where we talk with our minds, travel great distances without moving and disappear at will. Why do you think there are no Iridium or Rhodium supplements?" "Too heavy? Too rare? Too expensive?" offered Grace.

"That too. For the sole reason, that the powers that be don't want us to ingest it. The last thing that government and especially big pharma want, is a nation of healthy people. Like the banks with revolving credit. They are designed to keep us in debt, to keep us ill, to keep us suffering...to keep us scared."

Grace had had enough. "Oh, they are just conspiracy theories, Sherlock," she snapped. I didn't let her gain any headway in this argument. I was right and I stayed on her. "Like general and special relativity? Like evolution? These were theories twenty years ago, when nobody knew any better. Why do you think that natural remedies are referred to as a pseudo-science? Because nothing that occurs naturally can be patented. In order to be given to the public, a new drug has to be approved by the FDA, but first millions must be spent on research, and nobody is going to put that kind of money into something that they can't own outright and profit from."

Grace blew her cheeks out. "So, if my ideology is flawed, why exactly do you want my help?"

The truth left me cold. I could barely form the words. I walked over to her and clasped her by the shoulders.

"It's my mind palace," I said. "I'm locked out."

Grace looked at me thoughtfully. "How have you been locked out?" she asked.

I came from the kitchen with a small pile of white gloop on a saucer, essentially monatomic gold in powder form, mixed with water. I slurped it from the saucer, stood up tall and looked about me.... nothing. "I suspect it's that damn vaccination that Watson made me have. Whatever was in that syringe wasn't anything to do with covid.... if anything, ever was. I'm okay with remembering most things, things I expect to remember, but it's the material that I have only seen once and have filed away...I don't know where it is any more."

I turned to the wall again and thought quickly. "Right, we can't use technology for security reasons and for the simple reason that it won't work." I tapped my temple at Grace. "It's in there somewhere," I said, "I just have to get to it. We need books...old books...secret books, books that are kept in vaults, books you need gloves to read, like they have in the Vatican. Books we aren't meant to see."

Grace's face lit up. "I know someone who works at the Philosophical Research Society library in Kensington. It's full of Masonic, Rosicrucian and esoteric works; that might be a good start."

"Excellent," I said, "that's perfect."

"What are you thinking?" she asked.

"I'm going to read them. Then somewhere down the line, hopefully I can get back into my mind palace and scoop out the relevant information. It's just a matter of getting back in. If this concoction that I've just swallowed doesn't work, then only one thing will."

Grace turned from the wall. "And what's that?" she asked.

I looked at her with sadness. She knew immediately what I meant. "No, Sherlock," she scolded. "There must be another way. You can't keep running from your problems." I continued to gaze sadly at her. I thought of how little she really knew about me.

"Opium helps me confront and solve problems, my dear Grace, not run from them.

Hopefully it won't come to that." "What about planets?" she said.

I was right with her. "What about Gods? Aren't Gods and planets the same thing?"

"No, not at all."

I pulled my face. "Mercury, Venus, Mars, Jupiter...all planets and all Gods."

I felt a surge run through me. I started on the wall again with the pen. "Right, Mars, Venus, Earth, Mercury, Saturn, Jupiter, Neptune and Uranus...that's eight."

I put the headset on and saw the usual screen with the exploded motif, but now with the star in the middle, made up from the triangles. I took it off again.

"Okay let's try this. I'm going to say that the ice giants arrived too late and that Earth isn't a part of it." I started to write again. "So, let's say that the people worshipped, although the word is workship, you worked for your Gods. So we'll have Mars, Venus, Mercury, Jupiter, Saturn, the Sun and the Moon...seven planets."

Another whooshing sound came from the headset. I grabbed it and put it on. On the screen there was now a circle in the middle of the star and six others gathered around it." I was over the moon. I started to perform a crazy little dance around the room. "Woohoo," I exclaimed, "we have Chakras and planets...this is easy. Okay, what about the days of the week, while we're here. I wrote down the days of the week on the wall. Nothing. I thought I'd try the colors of the rainbow and though Grace had already listed them alongside the chakras, I listed them anyway. Silence from the headset.

Maybe it might not turn out to be that easy after all.

"What about places?" I said.

Grace started to gather her things together.

"Yes, places that I need to be," she said. "I have to go, Sherlock. I'll stop by the library and see if I can get those books. I'll bring back some food and toilet roll. Anything else you need?"

My mind was elsewhere. "Err...a burner phone," I answered, "and some Haribo Tangtsatics. In all events, we may not need the books. I'll probably have this finished by the time you get back. And under no circumstance are you to turn your phone back on until you are well away from the area. I don't want a surprise visit from my brother."

Grace slipped on her coat, grabbed her bag and gave me a peck on the cheek. She gave the wall one final look and chuckled at my first list, all crossed out. "See you later, Grumpy," she said.

I watched Grace leave from the window and watched her most of the way up the street. She didn't reach for her phone. I turned back to the wall. "Places. Places." I slumped down on my haunches and tried to digest the growing problem in front of me. Usually at this stage of a puzzle, I would start to recognize patterns. They would highlight themselves and jump out at me. At best, they fizzled and flickered, then just faded away. Somehow or other the vaccine I had been given had been intercepted and sabotaged, though it made absolutely no sense whatsoever for Dorian to set me such a complicated task, but then deprive me of the necessary faculties to solve it. Why would he do that? I made a mental note to check both the CCTV on Baker St and the one at the post office. I then wrote it down, just in case.

Again, I sat on the floor and stared at the wall, but nothing came of it and even though I had been quite convinced yesterday that a map of the world would be pertinent to the puzzle, and infuriatingly though it meant nothing to me now, I struggled with recalling even vaguely what it meant to me yesterday. My thoughts needed to be compartmentalized and the perfect way to do that would be to put my new meditation technique to use, to recognize, to acknowledge and to accept, but somehow, I thought that a barbecue wouldn't go down well right now with anybody, real or imagined. Till now, the test had been relatively straight forward, and two parts of the puzzle had been solved without too much ceremony, but I had a queasy feeling that I was soon going to be in serious trouble if I didn't move forward quickly. How could I advance? Where do I go from here? And what was all this to Mycroft? Why was he poking his nose in and what did he want with Dorian? I suspected that the extraordinary abilities that he possessed were no doubt being coveted by the secret services. Dorian's murderous ambition and blatant disregard for human life, coupled with his extraordinary ability to hop from one dimension to another was undoubtedly attractive for any government wishing to make great strides in the fields of war and counterintelligence. I had to find Dorian before Mycroft did, but more importantly I had to find Dorian before Mycroft found me.

A loud beep came from the headset, and I made a dive for it and rammed it on my head without further ado. The insignia burst forth for a moment and was then immediately replaced with a live video link. I recognized the setting immediately...we were back in the basement. As before, it took a few seconds for my eyes to adjust, but familiar shapes and shadows started to present themselves. The rough rock walls, the low ceiling with the gallery running around the top, the fast fingers of electricity that seemed to creep and crackle up through the rock and the table draped with the black cloth off to one side.

Two things were also very familiar, though not at all the same. Over to the other side of the cave was a bell-shaped object, again draped with a black cloth with three silver legs, suggestive of a tripod, protruding from below. And in the middle of the screen lay a man strapped to a table. He was lying face up, with yet another black cloth covering the lower part of his body. The man looked as stoic yet as scared as a man could possibly be under the circumstances. I had once asked a serial killer, what the difference was between fright and terror. He thought for a moment and then said to me. "Imagine that you had been unconscious and you woke to find yourself tied to a chair. Okay that's fright. Now imagine the same situation and you woke up tied to a chair, but the walls were covered in plastic sheeting. That's terror. Being tied to the chair would be bad enough, but the horror of knowing that diplomacy and discussion were not even on the cards and that you were about to be tortured and dismembered, would be acute and absolute.

As I watched him, his stoicism started to give way to precisely that feeling, and with very good reason. A low resonant vibration started to sound throughout the chamber, the rock wall away to the left gave way and through the opening appeared Dorian....and it wasn't the one from upstairs. He was bare-chested and wore a pair of loose black trousers. His upper body was decorated with symbols I didn't recognize, though my intensive study of the works of Irving Finkel told me they were closely related to the cylindrical texts of the Sumerians.

He started the slow walk to his captive and addressed him thus, "Born sick and ordered to be well," he said. "That's how it was put to the people, wasn't it? Born sick? In sin? I will have you know that human body is a remarkable machine, made from the finest materials to the highest specification. And believe it or not, designed to heal itself."

Dorian now stood in front of his beleaguered captive, their faces inches apart.

"Harry Adler. Founder and Managing Director of Seva

Pharmaceuticals...CEO of Whitestone PLC, Chief health advisor to the government, policy maker, member of congress, chairman of various boards and councils, blah blah fucking blah. Do you like money, Mr. Adler?"

I couldn't believe my ears. Irene's father. The man she had told me all about. The man she ran away from home because of...the man she hated, though I had never managed to find out why. Now I knew. I must admit that I felt a surge of excitement, borne out of a sense of justice for my ex-love and everything she must have gone through at the hands of this monster, as he stared back at Dorian, his eyes shot out with fear.

I knew by now that Dorian wasn't known for his patience and that ignoring the question would not go down at all well. "Answer the question, Mr. Adler," he said, "do you like money?"

I said that he said it, though not with his mouth. I watched closely and though I heard the words, I swear to God that Dorian's mouth didn't move when he uttered those words.

Harry Adler had noticed it too. His eyes widened in terror, and he looked frantically about him for an escape.

Dorian moved closer, their noses practically touching. Mr. Adler turned his face away, tears running down his cheeks.

"Please, whoever you are. I beg you. I'll do anything," he pleaded.

"You can start by answering my question."

"I'm a powerful man. I can give you whatever you want. I have money...lots of money. Just name your price. My legs feel numb."

Dorian smiled back, warming to the task ahead. "And in the process of accumulating all this wealth and power you think you have, you have destroyed millions of lives with your lies and your greed. You have set our plans back many years,

Mr. Adler. I can fix that. What I can't fix, is the minds of all the fucking children you raped."

He then moved over to the bell-shaped object and wheeled it over next to the gibbering old man. "There is a restaurant in Paris...Le Tour D'Argent...the silver tower, or the money tower if you want to use the slang, and they have an item on their menu for many years, which has been voted time and again as the best dish in the world. I have always wanted to try it."

He removed the black cloth to reveal a life-sized silver cloche about four foot high, with a wheel fixed to the top and a door in the side.

"Historically," he said, "the dish is made with duck, but I don't really care for the squawky little fuckers. It's a bit small for you and I didn't want you to be uncomfortable...." He turned a handle underneath the bench that Adler lay on and the whole thing flipped up and stood vertical. The black cloth that covered his bottom half fell away. "So, I cut your legs off!"

Harry Adler caught sight of his reflection in the cloche and began to seriously lose his mind. Not only had his legs been removed just below the groin, but his groin had also been removed too, just above the legs. A wretched howl came from him, as he took in his reduced presence.

"Please, not like this," he whimpered.

Dorian went up close again, his face inches from his captive. "Oh, don't worry," he said, "I'm not going to put you in like this.... I'm going to cook you first."

CHAPTER TEN

TO MATTER

The screen suddenly went black and the diabolical images were replaced by the exploded star and circle motif. I ripped the headset off and sat on the floor in shock. I had to marshal my thoughts as best I could. Irene's father was to be death number three, with the probable demise of the terrible Ellie-Mae somewhere down the line making it four. I didn't have much time to make the connection, find the pattern and anticipate Dorian's next step. We have a banker, a priest, a politician and a CEO. Who could possibly be next? How many more groups of seven could there be? And more importantly, how long would my memory, or lack of it, go on for? My mind raced. Places. But what type of places? And where?

I jumped to my feet, grabbed the marker and stared at the wall. What about countries? G7 countries. I listed them quickly and confidently. Seven countries...United Kingdom, United States, France, Germany, Japan, Canada and Russia. I put the headset on...nothing. Hmm. What about Italy? Italy's broke, but still in it. And no Russia. Or was it G8 now? Shit, I couldn't remember for the life of me.

I wrote another list. United Kingdom, United States, Italy, France, Germany, Japan and Canada. I was quite sure that the

European Union had been added recently, but try as I might, I couldn't get the list down to seven. I listed them anyway and donned the headset just to check. It wasn't countries. Ahh, what about continents? There were without a doubt seven of those. My confidence came back, and I fairly whizzed through the list, not letting my excitement spoil my handwriting and render it illegible. I figured that could count against me. Boom!...Australasia, Europe, Africa, North America, South America, Asia and Antarctica...headset...nothing. Bugger. I thought that was a nailed-on certainty.

Places, places. I began to stroll the room. I went to the window and looked up into the darkening sky for inspiration. Obviously, seven wonders of the world, how had I missed that. Now what were they? The places immediately listed far more than seven and danced around in my head. I started to list them as best I could. Pyramids of Giza, Hanging Gardens of Babylon, Temple of Artemis, Colossus of Rhodes. Lighthouse of Alexandria, Mausoleum at Halicarnassus, Statue of Zeus at Olympia. I didn't hear any whoosh from the headset but put it on anyway...I already had a back-up list ready to go. Nothing from the headset. I took it off again. They were the ancient wonders of the world; maybe it was the natural wonders.

I began my list. Aurora Borealis, Grand Canyon, Paricutin, Victoria Falls, Mount Everest, Harbor of Rio de Janeiro and the Great Barrier Reef. Supremely confident I donned the headset again...again nothing. I was beginning to lose my temper, surely it had to be.

"Fuckity fuckity fuck," I said. I took a deep breath and dug into my head a little deeper. Loitering on the periphery of my knowledge was the recollection that there was now in existence a new, updated seven wonders of the world. I told myself off and calmed myself down, before I tried to remember what they were. I stood at the wall; marker raised and took a few deep breaths. Okay, here we go. Slowly and calmly, I wrote them down as they came to me. Petra, Great Wall of China, Christ the Redeemer, The Colosseum, Machu Pichu, Chichen Itza and finally Taj Mahal. Surely, please. I have no more lists to give. It has to be right.

It has to be this...but it wasn't and it was at this point that I completely lost it.

Without a single thought for the consequences, I ripped off the headset and launched it at the wall, then chased it down and stomped it to pieces. "Fucking, cunting, bastard thing," I screamed, as I kicked the bigger pieces around the flat, until finally exhausted I slumped against the wall, sank down and sat on the floor. The realization of what I had done kicked in after I had thrown it, but I had already decided that the thing was irreparable before my foot was brought down in anger for the first time.

I concentrated on getting my breathing under control, as I sat and surveyed the destruction with abject sadness. The floor was covered with plastic, the wall was covered with lists, and I was the sum total of zero steps further on than I was when Grace left. Slowly I digested the enormity of what I had done. I reached up and felt my forehead; it was sticky. I rubbed my fingers together, sighed and stared at the wall, "bollocks," I said. In truth, I never said a word, I thought the word "bollocks", but I would have put my life on it there and then, that I had definitely heard myself say the word out loud. Something was happening to me and I didn't know what. I slipped on the spare dressing gown I had brought with me, filled my Vipe with a very heavy Indica and settled down in my armchair, facing the wall. In time I dozed.

When I say I dozed, what I actually did was skateboard off the end of the Universe. I dreamt that I was lying on a reclining black leather chair, from which I floated skywards and up through the ceiling. I started to pick up speed, twisting elegantly in the air, until a dark tunnel appeared and down it I went. The walls shimmered with electricity, and I trailed my fingers along them as I went. Eventually I dropped down into a dark, cavernous room and then completely underground, through a network of tunnels.

The sound of running water became rushing water and then became a deafening torrent until I plunged into it. All was silent for a few seconds and then I burst through the surface, out of the side of a hill and into a forest. Now through the trees, I started to climb, to twist and climb until I burst through the treetops and soared into the air, through the clouds and towards the stars into space. Images came thick and fast. I saw portals opening and closing, I saw pathways that led in two directions, ancient faces zipped past me both laughing and crying. I saw fractions and fractals, a web of shapes and words and numbers and I twisted through the lot. Deep harmonic sounds accompanied this magnificent journey through my dream, giving me a feeling of warmth and happiness, of safety and of hope.

As it started to get dark, I began to dream again about important sites around the world and had woken briefly and gone to the world map on the wall and decorated it with X's at the sites of ancient megalithic temples. I had then gone back to sleep.

I awoke with a start in my chair to the sound of the door being opened. It was Grace, pulling behind her a shopping basket. I was secretly furious that I had been wrenched from this beautiful world I had travelled to, but as I took stock of the beauty before me, dripping wet, with a huge smile on her face, I couldn't be mad for a second. Her smile disappeared as she looked at the destruction I had caused. She was visibly shaken. Her mood had completely gone.

"That easy, was it?" she asked.

I was ashamed of myself. How did I get so angry? Why

didn't I stop after the first throw? How had I let myself be overcome by my temper? And why hadn't I cleaned it up? I had no answer to any of these questions and more besides. I was heartbroken that I had upset her and probably wasted her journey. I looked up at her.

"It's all up to me now," I said. I jumped to my feet and glared at the wall.

"How did you do that?" Grace asked, as I readied the marker.

"I've been getting up from chairs for as long as I can remember," I replied.

I felt her eyes drilling into the side of my head. "Your mouth didn't move," she said.

"Don't really need it for getting off chairs."

I knew exactly what she meant, but until I had deduced what changes were happening in my body, I wasn't really ready to get into it. Grace started to unpack the books she had brought. She stacked them neatly and carefully on the table.

"Wow!" I said, "what books did you get?" making a disrespectful grab at them.

"Oh, I got quite a selection," she answered, "I got a few by Manly. P. Hall, a couple by some woman called Madame Blavatsky. Apparently, she knew a lot about the early history of humankind...the forbidden kind. I have books on the Olmec, the Toltec and the Aztecs, two books on giants, one on the Sumerians and one on megalithic temples."

"Brilliant!" I exclaimed, "that's exactly what I'm working on right now." I shuffled across to the map of the world.

"Right, I've got the big ones in...the obvious ones. We have Stonehenge here, Great Pyramid here, Easter Island here, the Pyramid of the Sun over there. I know there's one here in Cambodia and one in Turkey or Syria over here somewhere." I turned to Grace. "Did you get the phone?" I asked.

Grace fished the phone from her bag and handed it to me.

"It's one of my old ones," she said, "but I got a new sim card for it." She gave a long last look at the wall. "Right, Sherlock, I'm going to leave you to it; I have classes tonight. But don't worry, I'm doing them from home. I'll pop by again tomorrow and see how you're getting on. I take it you'll be here?"

"If I manage to figure out how he's travelling, then no...if I don't then yes."

Grace zipped up her shopping cart and started to head for the door. She produced a bag of Haribo's from her coat pocket and handed them to me. "Tangtastic? she said. I wasn't listening but I did grab the sweets from her and opened them immediately.

"Splendiferous," I answered. I knew immediately that she was talking about the name of the sweets, but I just left it there, just as I knew that she had glanced back up at the wall, had seen my first lists all crossed out, including the seven dwarves before she opened the door and said, "Bye, Grumpy."

That particular evening flew by in a blur of fractured dreams and mini revelations. For the most part, nothing happened. As humans are inclined to do, I looked for order in the puzzle, trying to force it into a pattern, but for the life of me I couldn't get past the lists, however the second I closed my eyes, my head filled with magic and possible solutions. One particular instance stood out in the night; one that had me staring at the wall in disbelief, then dancing like a dervish around the flat. It was right after this momentous breakthrough that my body finally let go and allowed me to eventually get some rest. I drifted away with a smile on my face, optimistic for tomorrow. I imagined the look on Grace's face, when I presented her with this mind-blowing breakthrough.

Sadly, things didn't turn out as I had hoped, and I was catapulted from my sleep by the sound of my phone ringing. It could only be Grace. I launched myself from the armchair I was crumpled on top of and made a dive for the window. Throwing it open, I was met with the image of Grace, on her phone; she stood in the street looking up at my window.

"Turn your phone off," I hissed. "Turn your bloody phone off."

I raced downstairs and almost yanked the front door off its hinges. Grace gave me an embarrassed smile, as I grabbed her by the arm and dragged her into the hallway.

"Why didn't you take the key?" I asked, as we trudged up the staircase.

"Because I was gone for the night. You might have wanted to go for a walk, or whatever private detectives do. I did send you a text and threw stones at your window. You must have been in a deep sleep."

I opened the door to the flat and Grace's face fell in horror. The place was not only upside down, inside out and back to front, but was also torn to shreds. I stared at the carnage with her, shocked myself by what lay before me. The precious books were strewn across the floor and covered every inch of it. Pages had been ripped out and stuck to the wall. One page had been made into an airplane. Beside me, Grace began to choke. She stared, open-mouthed with one hand on the wall, holding herself up.

"Oh my God, Sherlock...what have you done?"

"What I have done, my dear Grace, is discovered how he is travelling...sit down, sit down."

Shell shocked, Grace perched herself on the edge of a chair and gazed at the floor with a sadness I had never seen in anyone, but I was convinced that I could win her over in no time. I grabbed the marker and went to the map.

"Okay, originally, we had Rapa Nui, or Easter Island here...Stonehenge, Great Pyramid, Stone Circles of South Africa, Angkor Wat and Teotihuacan, Pyramid of the Sun over here. Right, let's draw a line from the Pyramid of the Sun to the Great Pyramid. You go through the ancient city of Cusco in Peru, through Coelcene, the Stonehenge of Brazil, Nagayene in Senegal, Tazanu in Niger, through the Great Pyramid and straight through to Southern Turkey and the impressive recently discovered Gobekli Tepi. Again, let's go from the Pyramid of the Sun, again through the Great Pyramid and through to the sunken temple of Yonaguni off the coast of Japan. Go from the Stone Circles of South Africa, through Tazanu...Stonehenge. Go from Stonehenge, through Gobekli Tepi.... Angkor Wat." I turned excitedly to Grace, who was still in shock. "Grace, there are dozens and dozens of them and they all line up. They are built...."

"On ley lines," Grace finished off, without emotion.

"Yes, but bigger. Have you heard of Torus energy? Earth's electro-magnetic field...rises out of the top, comes back around, and essentially feeds itself and just keeps going."

Grace sounded tired and bored, though instinct told me that she was still hurt. "The human biofield is the same," she said. "Subtle energies rise up from the head, circles back around the body, in the shape of an apple. That's what auras are, electro-magnetic energy."

I was delighted. "The same," I exclaimed, "Then I started to look at the shapes that they formed on the map. Triangles... lots of triangles and they started to look familiar. Now let's go back to these circles. It isn't seven...well it is. You take one circle and you can only fit six circles of the same size around it. Six around the one."

Grace was still sad. "Okay," she said, not looking at me, or indeed at anything.

"Like a cluster of cells, or atoms...I sat and stared at this for hours...and it finally hit me. I took the triangles from the map, and I placed them over the clusters of circles."

Grace gritted her teeth, as I dropped to my knees and started to scrabble around in the books again, flinging them left and right. I found what I was looking for and held it up to her.

"And I found this!"

Grace looked from the book to the wall and back again. "What is it?"

"Metatron's Cube!" I announced gleefully. "A geometric design that contains all of the platonic shapes. Tetrahedron, dodecahedron, la la la...the 3d shapes. Plato described them as the building blocks of all matter in the Universe...water crystals, snowflakes, DNA, everything!"

Grace looked puzzled. "I know who Plato is," she said, "but who is Metatron?"

I started to get excited again, now that Grace had softened a little. "Sounds like a transformer, doesn't he? He was an angel. Plato described him as the scribe of the Gods and his job was to guard heavenly secrets."

From out of nowhere, a knot developed in my stomach, and I had an unreasonable feeling of impending doom. I grabbed the burner phone and went to the window. I threw it open and gave a short, sharp whistle, then ducked back inside.

"Thanks to your impatience, our location is no longer a heavenly secret."

Grace raised her eyebrows at me and I knew why. I was the one who had just destroyed a trolley full of priceless books and at the same time, the library's trust in her, though not her trust in me. Yet here she was in my bad books once more and yet again getting another unwarranted telling off. She protested weakly.

"I was trying to get in touch with you, Sherlock; I had to turn it on."

The feeling of doom continued to grow. I picked up the pace and began to gather my things together.

"In the dark and grimy streets of London, there is still only one way to send a message. Give me your phone."

"And how's that?"

A whistle came from the street. "By urchin," I said.

I leaned from the window and throwing down the phone, I addressed the two lads who had appeared below. "I have put a number in there and turned the volume down. Go over the bridge, to the other side of the river. Call the number and hide the phone. And make sure that nobody sees you."

I turned back to Grace. "What are you going to do now?" she said.

"I think I should be doing the same thing as my brother, Mycroft. He is looking for you to get to me and I should be looking for someone else to get to Dorian."

"Who?"

"Number five."

Grace ignored me and started to rescue what she could from the books she had brought. She looked distraught again.

I crouched at the window and looked out across the river.

On the other side of the bridge two black Range Rovers appeared and skidded to a halt. Several men in black exited from the cars and started to run about aimlessly checking doors and alleyways. I watched them wander in circles for a few minutes looking lost. I took out my phone, turned it on and while looking at the wall, started to text. Tiny sobs came from Grace as she tried in vain to put the pages of a book back together, then put them in her trolley.

"I'm in so much trouble with the library," she said. The librarian is a very close friend of mine. Well, she was. I'm going to leave you to it, Sherlock. I don't want any part of it. I can help you with your chaotic life, but I can't live it with you. And the phone rule just applies to me I see. And where have they gone with my phone?"

I carried on with my text. I turned briefly to her. "No, you can't leave yet," I said. "My brother has the area surrounded, and this phone is untraceable. I am only texting to one number, which is also untraceable. Last night I was looking for ancient sites in Greece...harder than you may think." I picked up a page that I had torn from one of the books, and I found this! The Antikythera Mechanism...thousands of years old, found at the turn of the twentieth century on a sunken Roman wreck. It's a mechanical computer made of bronze, and it predicts the movements of certain stars and the planets, according to the month and, seeing as I don't have the headset anymore, it gave me an idea."

I finished the text and took a photo of the wall, sent it and then turned the phone off and placed it on the table. My heart sunk a little, as I watched Grace hopelessly trying to retrieve the precious books. I knelt beside her and started to help when my phone beeped. I stared at the phone and then at Grace.

"I had just turned that off," I said.

"You couldn't have done. Probably a reply to whatever you've just sent."

"I definitely just turned it off," I protested.

I picked the phone up and looked at the screen. A message had come through...it said:

"What we gave you, what you took. You can see what's missing, if you dare to look."

I showed the message to Grace, then sat on the floor with my back to the wall and stared into space. "He's back," I said.

"But who's we?"

I jumped to my feet, grabbed the marker and addressed the wall. "Right, I'm going to pick seven megalithic sites. I began to write them down. "Gobekli Tepi, Teotihuacan, Pyramid of Giza, Stone Circles of South Africa, Angkor Wat, Stonehenge and Easter Island." I looked at my phone, but it made not a sound. "And *we*, I believe, is whoever Dorian represents...this committee or Council of Seven, who are probably Gods...give me seven Gods."

"Egyptian?"

"No...it'll be earlier. Probably Sumerian...the chapter before. Give me seven."

Grace promptly found the chapter on Sumerian Gods and as she recited them, I listed them on the wall. I may have known them previously, but with my memory running at reduced capacity, as it stood, I had never heard of any of the names before.

"Enzu, Nabu, Shamash, Marduk, Anu, Enki and Enlil," I said, then stepped back and looked at the names.... nothing came.

"I remember that story," said Grace.

"Which story?"

"The oldest story ever told, the Epic of Gilgamesh."

I had never heard of it and I told her so.

"It's the original story of Noah and the Great Flood. Anu was their father. One wanted to save the planet and the other wanted to destroy it."

"Anu was whose father?"

"Enki and Enlil's," she said. "The warring brothers." An explosion went off in my brain.

"Of course," I blurted out. "That's who he is."

I turned my attention back to the wall. "But what has he got against this lot? We have a banker, a priest, a CEO and most likely a politician. Who are the other three and what connects them all? They must be part of a secret club or an organization."

Grace pulled her face. "What kind of club?"

My heart leapt, then promptly sank. "What's the worst thing you can think of?"

Grace had obviously decided that she needed to go. She

wearily fished a bunch of crushed grapes from the trolley and threw them in the bin. She sighed heavily.

"I had forgotten about these," she said. "Well, the books can't get any more ruined than they are right now. I have to go, Sherlock. I can't stay here. Hopefully, I still have a life to lead."

"No," I insisted, "you can't leave yet."

I started to draw clusters of circles on the wall, one in the middle and six around them. "Don't go yet. There's a secret way out of here, I'll get the urchins to guide you out safely. "What they gave us...what who gave us? What did the Gods give us? Get the book on the Sumerians back out. They left thousands of cuneiform texts...the first bill of sale, the first alphabet. What else did they give to us?"

Grace picked her way through the sticky pages of said book. As she recited the following to me, I put them into their respective cluster of circles. I needed seven clusters of seven, made up so far of occupation of victim, God, planet, megalithic site and chakra. In cluster one I wrote, banker, Enzu, Venus, Teotihuacan and Root. In cluster two I wrote, Priest, Nabu, Mars, Stone Circles of South Africa and Sacral. Cluster three, Judge,

Shamash, Mercury, Easter Island and Solar Plexus. Cluster four, CEO, Marduk, Saturn, Angor Wat and Heart. Cluster five, Politician, Enki, Jupiter, Gobekli Tepi and Throat.

Cluster six, first circle blank, Enlil, Moon, Great Pyramid and Third Eye and Cluster Seven was blank, Anu, Sun, Stonehenge and Crown. It was all starting to make some sense. Grace found something in the book and a tiny bit of excitement crept back into her voice. I stood back and beamed at the wall.

"Okay, here we are," she said. "Wow, it looks like we got everything from the Sumerians...well, seven things anyway."

I nodded. "Brilliant," I said, "one by one, what are they?"

"Arithmetic."

I put that in Cluster One with the banker.

"Geometry."

For now, I put that in Cluster Four with the CEO.

"Grammar."

This went into Cluster Three.

"Rhetoric."

That obviously went in Cluster Five with the politician.

"Astronomy." Cluster Two.

"Music."

I added this to Cluster Six and stood back and stared at the list. "And the last one will be logic," I said.

Grace smiled at me finally. "Yes."

I stood with the marker raised. Slowly and purposefully, I wrote the word "Singer" in Cluster Six.

For no reason, other than to say it, I was briefly overtaken by the spirit of John Cleese in The Life of Brian. "Alright," I said, "but apart from geometry, logic, astronomy, arithmetic and music, what have the Sumerians ever done for us?"

I didn't bother to look at Grace for a reaction, let alone a laugh. "Never mind," I said. I went to the window, threw it open and whistled for an urchin. I took a twenty-pound note from my pocket, scrunched it up and dropped it out of the window. I then turned to Grace.

"Right, time to go. Go back to your normal life, I'll be in touch, don't try to contact me. If anyone asks, you haven't seen me, nor do you have any plans to see me. The urchins will get you back to Camden. And Grace?"

She forced a smile. "Yes?"

"I'm sorry about the books."

There was a coded tap at the door and when I opened it, an urchin stood there in hopeful, ragged splendor. I wheeled Grace's trolley to him, gave Grace a quick peck on the cheek and closed the door. Before I did, I noticed that the grapes had left a trail of sticky juice on the floorboards in the hallway. I knew I had to move quickly. I took one last look at the map and noticed that there was a large space, where no triangles met. I grabbed the marker again and drew a line from Yonaguni, through the Great Pyramid and out into the Atlantic Ocean. Surely there had to be something there...maybe Atlantis.

Out of interest I extended the line all the way up to the East coast of Alaska. Then I went cold. I had an unnerving feeling that the walls were closing in. I hastily threw everything I needed into my backpack and made my way through the hole behind the wardrobe on the upper landing, that led through to next door. With some effort I pulled the wardrobe back against the wall, then made my way through the derelict buildings and out through a coal shed onto the street beside the river. I had concluded my escape from the shithole. Creeping stealthily over Greenwich bridge near the O2, I hailed a taxi and directed it to Holland Park.

CHAPTER ELEVEN

THE HALLS OF AMENTI

My taxi driver wasn't too pleased about my instructions to wait, but after being given a bunch of money, he changed his tune and decided to tell me jokes and talk about football, neither of which I had the slightest interest in. We waited almost half an hour, by which time the meter was displaying all kinds of numbers. The taxi driver sprang to life though, when I spotted Elli-Mae Price's opulent gates bend open and her SUV backed out onto the road. She gunned the engine and roared off up the wet street, with the taxi keeping a fair distance behind. After about ten minutes, her car veered off the main road and instead took roads of ever-receding tarmac, until suddenly out of the blue, her brake lights came on. The car made an aggressive U-turn and hurtled back towards us. Doing the same would no doubt have made us more conspicuous than we already were, so I instructed the driver to continue until her lights were out of sight and then we stopped.

Ahead in the gloaming, I could make out a private entrance into a wood and the shape of a triangular building hidden therein. I gave the driver some more money and then exited the cab.

I watched the lights of the taxi fade into the distance and found myself quite alone on a dirt path, almost pitch black, deathly quiet and only the smell of the forest. The road eventually gave way to a dirt path, which was straddled by tire tracks on the grass either side by an off-road vehicle. A couple of hundred yards further on, the path broke out into a perfectly circular clearing, inside which stood a semi-subterranean pyramid, made of what I couldn't immediately discern, though as I got closer I realized it was obviously a stone material of some description and though it had been raining for hours, it glistened in the moonlight with something other than water.

I ducked into the bushes at the side of me and took a better look at the layout of the building and tried to figure out my best approach to it unseen and unheard. Sadly, I couldn't do both, so I forewent the chance of being seen for the chance of being heard and picked my way blindly through the bushes round to the rear of the property. There were two entrances I could see, and both sloped down dramatically from the outer wall to what I imagined to be the center of the pyramid. I wouldn't have to imagine for very long.

In recent years, my untimely death and subsequent resurrection has unfortunately become back page news. I have drowned twice, been shot twice, faked my death once and had three overdoses, which makes me somewhat of an authority on the procession to the other side. I should really have a season ticket. Suffice to say I know death, and this wasn't it. No lights, no tunnels, no tribunal; nothing about it was the same apart from the color. Wherever I was, I was warm, calm and happy to be there. Yet again I found myself twisting through the forest, bursting through the canopy into the air and once more on an inter-dimensional flight of magic and wonder, until finally I flipped in the air and barreled towards Earth again. I came in low over London, skimming the treetops in Regents Park, down Baker Street and down through the ceiling of 221B and into my bed.

My eyelids sprang open and I lay for a second, rigid, arms by my sides in my own bed, taking stock of my surroundings. All was as it should be, apart from me not remembering being there. My memory had really taken an absolute pasting. I clearly remembered being in a taxi, following Ellie-Mae Price into the countryside. I also distinctly remember walking through a forest that surrounded a pyramid. Or did I? I did a quick body scan and then tentatively got out of bed. I was fully dressed, though that was nothing out of the ordinary. I was rested, so I had slept. I stood in the center of my living room and slowly and carefully looked around. It was my flat alright, but something was off, so I checked for details. My bedside clock seemed to think that it was morning, but quickly I began to realize what was wrong.

If I had spent the night here and this was now daybreak, then obviously Mrs. Hudson hadn't been in yet. And if Mrs. Hudson hadn't been in yet, then why was my apartment so tidy? There wasn't a thing out of place. If my mind serves me correctly, I have yet to wake up to a tidy apartment...there was always some kind of destruction in evidence, testament to the night before. Either I had just arrived, or Mrs. Hudson had just left, but neither of these statements I held to be true. Maybe Mrs. Hudson could help. The clock on the mantlepiece said it was 06.15 and though I was fully aware that Mrs. Hudson didn't get going till 7, I needed her here right now to fill in the blanks for me. I strode to the window, to throw a bit more light on the matter.

“Mrs. Hudson? Mrs. Hudson! I shouted, yanking back the curtains...behind which, was a brick wall. I rushed to the door, knowing my hallway wouldn't be behind it and I was right, it wasn't...but somebody's was. A long, dark corridor stretched away before me, black and picked out in neon blue.

To my right was a gallery, that overlooked the cavernous room I had seen on the two occasions on the headset, but now I got to see it in all its terrible glory. Around twenty meters in diameter, the rough-cut walls rose above my head and tapered to a point some thirty meters further up. The walls were of basalt or mica and flickered with blue fingers of electricity. A low hum vibrated throughout the building. In the center of the structure were seven crystals about a meter high, all stood on their ends in a tight circle. Up ahead along the wall to my left were three doors. I approached the first door, which was open wide. I stood in the doorway and looked in on an elegant female quarters. Well aware that I was being watched and allowed to roam, I stepped into the room.

Expensive dresses hung in the wardrobe, the whole theme of the room was renaissance Italy, with dark woods and heavy brocades and chamber music seemed to seep through the walls. A TV ran silently in the corner, playing some nondescript daytime show. There was a sofa in front of the TV, on which was strewn a woolen throw and on a side table next to it, was a full glass and an empty bottle of gin.

In the center of the room was a huge unmade four-poster bed. This room had obviously been in use, though wasn't any more and was unlikely to be in the future. I knew this owing to the large blood stain in the center of the bed. I knew immediately that I was too late and that I was indeed standing in the room where Judge Rosalind Parker had met her end. The violence surprised me, as I was under the assumption that the utmost care was to be taken with the female victims.

I exited the room and pressed on. The next door was half open, inviting me to explore further. I pushed the door open with a finger and looked at a room in total contrast to the previous one. This room was pristine. The furniture was all bold, block colors with straight lines and sharp edges. It had an ultra-modern, though impersonal feeling to it. The bed was a minimalist box of light pine, was exquisitely made and turned down. This room was ready for someone and judging by the overall feel and taste of the room, I guessed that this room was ready for a certain Ellie-Mae Price. I left the room and edged further down the corridor. I appeared in the doorway of the kitchen and sitting at a table was Dorian. It took a few seconds for me to take a flash bomb scan of his and now my surroundings, which without removing his eyes from mine, he allowed me to do.

He had a superbly poised head, which was round and tanned and smooth. He had the eyes of a hunter, blue and sharp and fixed on his subject, like a kestrel. His mouth was well-stocked and in top order; it was a mouth that was generous and ready to smile. Well established laughter lines ran from his eyes down to the corner of his mouth and gave him the appearance of a human cheetah. His manicured hands moved smoothly over the fabric of his clothes, as he crossed his legs, folded his hands together and smiled at me.

His suit was exquisite and made me unreasonably angry. Judging by the soft shoulders and extra material around the chest, it was ostensibly Florentine or Neapolitan and after further inspection and noting a small motif on the cuff, I deduced it was made by non-other than Michele Marinaro, the bright eyed and slick fingered protege of the legendary Loris Vestrucci of Florence.

My own suits had hitherto been crafted by Edward Sexton, former business partner of the inimitable tailor to the stars Tommy Nutter of Saville Row and though this relationship had been as carefully crafted by my father as one of Nutter's quirky, structured English cuts, the whole thing had been blown to bits by Mycroft and a toe-to-toe screaming match over the correct shade of a pocket square, the result being that my brother had had his picture pinned to the wall, as if he'd passed counterfeit twenties in a pub and none of my present family, nor any from the future were welcome in that establishment until further notice.

I had decided to get away from the stifled constraints of the English tailor and after visiting several ateliers in Napoli and Florence had finally settled on Sartoria Vestrucci. That's why I was angry. His shoes were a classic Oxford brogue, that I thought at first was the work of Stefano Bemer, who's shoes I had several pairs of, though I hadn't noticed the tweed golosh on the outside, which I now saw when he crossed his legs, telling me instantly that the shoes were a playful version of a near-on two-hundred-year-old design by the great shoemaker John Lobb.

I silently applauded him on his taste, but my mood soured again when his shirt cuff rode back and I noticed his watch. Now I, as the self-proclaimed Master of Deduction, must admit right here that this mantle was appropriated by me after meeting watchmaker extraordinaire Frank Muller, the self-styled Master of Complication. I loved his title and I loved the intricacies of his timepieces. I was the proud owner of the Aeternitas Mega, his most complicated watch to date, but while that two-million-pound gift gathered dust somewhere in my apartment, I subconsciously flicked my shirt cuff over my idiot-proof Patek Phillipe in embarrassment when I saw what he was wearing on his wrist.

There are two stories to this watch, the first is that this timepiece is the only one of its kind in existence and the second story I heard is that there have been only five made. Whatever the correct number, I had never seen one in real life and as it was a pocket watch, I never expected to see one on the wrist.

I glanced and I glanced again, but there was no doubt, I was indeed looking at a Vacherin Constantin Flying Tourbillon Napoleon Jacquemart, the rarest and with almost three thousand components, the most complicated watch on Earth.

If I was saddened, angered and humiliated by the things he was wearing that I could see, nothing was to prepare me for my next humbling, for the things I could not, well not with my eyes.

In all matters of style and taste I have proudly and now maybe stupidly acquired the moniker of afficionado and even some areas snob, which I don't mind in the least, though my historical and much heralded knowledge of wine would soon be unmasked as the reader will discover in following lines. My seemingly unrivalled penchant for fine clothes and timepieces had been matched, surpassed and laid bear with ease and now my last area of expertise was to go through the ringer and would almost bring me to tears. That area was parfum and fragrance and as I stood gazing at my host, my carefully chosen, season-dependent, weather-assisted, mood-related Boadicea the Victorious, turned to vinegar on my skin and seeped weakly from my pores like a Chinese knockoff, as I slowly and secretly breathed in.

It couldn't be, but yes it could and yes it certainly was. The scent must have been applied in the last ten minutes, as the instant notes were without doubt only one of two. First came Italian bergamot and Sicilian lemon and in another hour that scent could go one of two ways and develop Cedar Wood and Patchouli, later showing up as Amber and Vanilla and would be the Xantor.

On the other hand, and I could feel it before I smelled it, it could go Lavender, Patchouli and Jasmine, till the night brought on Amber, Musk and Frankincense. It wasn't just the smell of Jasmine that I adored, but more specifically the memory of what the smell meant to me. It took me back to the Cote D'Azur. I was transported back to a regular trip I used to make between Cannes and Genoa, with a suicidal Italian friend of mine. When I say suicidal, the man wasn't depressed in the slightest, rather I attribute this adjective to all male Italian drivers, where the general objective for them being behind the wheel, was to catch the car in front. These hair-raising journeys were given added zest and danger with the fact that on one side of the twisting road was the dizzying aroma of the endless fields of Jasmine Grandiflorum and Centifolia Roses of Grasse and on the other, the vertiginous drop onto sharp rocks and the gently crashing waves of the Mediterranean.

The smell of the flowers came from one side, the ocean breeze from the other and they met in the middle, right under my nose and I would just close my eyes, lean back and breathe.

It was a wonderful time of my life, where I cared not one jot for much of anything, including my own life that hung in the balance on every one of those trips. Again here, my life hung in the balance, but like the snob I am, I quietly congratulated myself on my deduction of Dorian's parfum, it was without a doubt the Siskor and not the Xantor. I didn't enjoy the moment for long though, as I realized with a painful melancholy, that if I could have been taken away on a memory, on that particular memory, taking that twisting road from France to Italy, I would close my eyes and drive past the Roses and the Jasmine of Grasse. I would also drive past the headquarters of the man who's hands had crafted this unforgettable scent, the perfumier, Henry Jacques.

I tried to remember the layout and contents of the kitchen, without taking my eyes from his. The room was unremarkable, save for it being made totally from marble and chrome. There were no appliances to speak of, though a fridge and an oven were clearly visible and were again not worthy of note, though I did notice that the oven was at least three times the size of any domestic model. A low vibration seemed to reverberate throughout the whole structure and over the top of that, a harp concerto tiptoed its way around the house. I felt in no danger, while at the same time, was acutely aware that I was in the presence of immense power. Dorian's smile was wide and genuine. His eyes twinkled.

"Glad you could make it, Sherlock," he said, "what did you think of your room?" Careful not to stumble, I paused before answering.

"Very impressive," I said. "Must have took a while to get it just right."

My host seemed genuinely pleased with this. "Thank you, I worked hard on it. Apparently one of my dinner guests can't make it, so we can change the format up a bit."

I guessed that he was talking about a certain politician.

"She has gotten away twice," I said. He waved it away. "I did say that everything happens in twos, Sherlock. No doubt I will catch up with her soon. I need her for energy."

The answer seemed clear to me. "So why don't you just go and get her?"

At this he laughed. "Because I need the energy to do so. Imagine that you have no milk for your coffee, but you need the coffee first, in order to go and get the milk. Ever been there?"

"I drink tea...without milk," I replied somewhat too smugly.

"Ah yes," You have given it up...along with opium, tobacco and masturbation." He looked straight into my eyes. "Commendable."

I hope the reader will forgive me for choosing not to disclose this particular nugget of information and I see no need to embarrass myself further with any more details on the subject. My host took a similar view on the matter and thankfully limited my discomfort to that one brief moment.

"There isn't much I don't know, Sherlock," he said, "please sit down."

I took a seat opposite Dorian, trying to act as cool as possible. My mind was still racing over the uncomfortable truth about my bedroom habits.

He stared at me intently. "Don't worry, I'm not judging you. You're so close, Sherlock," he said, "I have had to sprinkle a few obstacles in your way, for fear of you solving the whole thing too quickly, which is testament to your power of deduction. You wouldn't want it too easy, would you? Thanks to your temper, I don't feel so bad about giving you a few clues along the way. I hope you haven't given up cheese as well, though I'm afraid I don't have any Hobnobs to go with them."

Again. Mind blown. Where the hell was he getting this information from? Even Mrs. Hudson and Dr. Watson were ignorant of this detail. I finally came to the horrible, inevitable truth that he might actually know what I was thinking. For no reason, or maybe indeed for that exact reason, Dorian smiled.

I didn't take my eyes from his for a second. "Obstacles," I said, "like the DMT in the headset?"

He beamed across the table at me and I pushed on. "And whatever you swapped out the vaccine for, to make me lose my memory."

He laughed out loud. "Oh, that wasn't me, that was your brother," he said, "though I must admit, that it did suit me fine to have you locked out of your mind palace for a while. Right now, I want to take you to a place...where senses collide. Apart from your questionable attempt at pairing lobster with tomatoes, I have never known you to eat two foods that actually go together."

He flashed a hand at the table. There were maybe ten different cheeses on display and probably the same number of opened bottles of red wine. Dorian took a cheese knife and selected one. from which he cut two slices. He then selected a wine and poured two small glasses.

"Let's start with an easy one," he said. "Take a bite of this cheese, chew it fourteen times, swallow it, wait three seconds, suck it through your teeth and then try this wine. A Sasakia '87...just before it starts its decline."

I did exactly as he said. I bit, chewed, swallowed, picked the wine up, sucked the cheese through my teeth and tasted the wine. I closed my eyes, as the flavors spread around my palate, up through my synapses and danced into my head, where they arrived as one and gave me what I can only describe as a brain orgasm. A warm sensation crept down my spine, then shot back up and exploded in my head. I opened my eyes and stared at him.

"Wow," I said.

Dorian was immensely pleased. "Excellent," he exclaimed. "That's umami...that's an easy one." He chose another wine and poured it again in two fresh glasses. "Now, taste this one and tell me what you see."

I put the proffered glass to my lips and as before, I ran the wine around my mouth before swallowing slowly. I wanted to look and sound like a wine snob, an aficionado, a cultured and well-travelled member of society. In short, I wanted to please my host but try as I might to search for exotic and inventive superlatives, I couldn't. I wanted to tell him about hints of juniper and tobacco, with mahogany undertones, but sadly nothing came. I felt and probably looked confused and quickly out of my depth. I was a wine snob to most of the people I knew, but not to this man. I stared at my host.

"I'm not getting anything," I said. "Blackberries," I offered.

Dorian looked back at me patiently. "Wrong," he said. "Not what you taste. Tell me what you see. Sometimes we can see things better when we close our eyes." I put the glass to my lips once more and closed my eyes.

"Now tell me what you see."

I was struggling again. I expected to be inundated with

bunches of dark fruits and dark woods, but I was sadly mistaken. I was wary of trying to force a thought, so relaxed my mind and let the answers come. They didn't. I opened my eyes again and stared blankly at him.

"I'm sorry, nothing's coming," I said. "I just see flames."

Dorian was overjoyed. He clapped his hands together in delight.

"Excellent!" he exclaimed. "Nappa Valley Merlot 2006." He leaned across the table towards me. "The crop burned down."

He jumped to his feet and opened a set of double doors, that led into an adjacent room.

"Follow me," he said. "Still play the violin?"

I got to my feet and followed him into a room that could only be described as a museum of strings. There were instruments from all countries and all eras. I looked around in wonder.

"Err, no not really," I replied. "I've had tinnitus for the past few years; I can't really hear the notes anymore. I only really played it to think and to mess with my neighbors."

Dorian took a violin from the wall and handed it to me. "Here," he said, "I think it needs tuning."

I plucked a few strings and ran a scale or two on it and then held it out to him. "Nothing wrong with that. It's perfectly in tune."

My host smiled at me. "Well how do you know, if you can't hear the notes?" he said. He had a point.

"You can't hear the notes when it's tuned to 440, but your body doesn't resonate at that frequency...it's 432. Tune it to the same frequency as your body."

He went to a drawer in a side unit and handed me an autotuner. I tuned the violin to the desired frequency, handed Dorian the tuner back, put the instrument under my chin and started to play. I tried one of my favorites, not thinking for one second that anything would be different...how wrong I was. I played slowly, unsurely, like I was holding a violin for the first time...I played the notes and when I played them, I felt them, and when I felt them, I heard them. One after another, note after note came easily and clearly and the wonder began to grow in me. My confidence came back, my sadness came back, and through it my happiness and my love of music.

I felt a little more adventurous and though I wanted to try a Caprice, I didn't have the confidence in front of this guy, so I settled for the G Major section of a Beethoven concerto. I played with growing relish and abandon. I was punting on the Cherwell back in Oxford, gliding under the Magdalen Bridge, lamenting lost loves and broken dreams. Tears streamed unchecked down my face and though I was vaguely aware that I was crying in front of a grown man who I had never met before, I didn't care. I was gone, I was lost in the music, and I felt like in all senses of the word that I was home.

Dorian had his eyes open when I had started to play and closed them when I started to cry, such was his understanding of the human condition. Finally, he opened his eyes again and walked over to a Theremin, that was standing in the corner of the room. He positioned himself, reached out to the instrument and started to play along with me, his mournful sounds harmonizing beautifully with mine. The two instruments found each other in the air and swirled and wrapped around each other, soared skywards and let each other go again, weaving an intricate fugue in the air between us, a beautiful dance, a mating ritual, a love affair, bound by frequency and vibration.

Dorian suddenly dropped his arms and the sound from the Theremin stopped. I stopped playing too and wiped my face with the back of my sleeve. I felt exhilarated, and a little bit silly.

"Would you like to try?" he said.

I handed him the violin, which he replaced on the wall and approached the Theremin. I had seen people play it before and understood the basic concept of it enough to get a sound out of it, but never a tune. I took a deep breath and waved my hands in the general direction of it, causing a low grinding sound to emanate from my left hand and a high-pitched squeal from my right. I found some kind of range and tried to gesticulate within the parameters they set, though sadly what was formed could hardly be called music. Dorian was more than generous with his comments as he stood in front of me, transfixed.

"Not bad," he said. He was right, it was much worse than that. "Now try playing it with your hands behind your back."

What on Earth was the man talking about? I could barely force a note with two hands and could probably only muster a tune from it with a few more hands, not less, let alone none. I did as he said and put my hands behind my back and as expected the damn thing fell silent. I knew what was required of me, so I focused on the instrument and at the same time began the pulse in my solar plexus. The pulse came and when I let it go, the familiar feeling of warmth and unfettered love began to shoot up my spine, down my legs, across my chest and down my arms. As the sensation crept up my throat, I raised my head and opened my mouth to allow it to leave me and as it did so, it was accompanied by a rather embarrassing squeak from the Theremin. I lost my focus and the instrument stopped dead. I meekly stepped away as Dorian approached it, his hands clasped behind his back.

He closed his eyes and as I watched on in pure amazement, he began to play expertly and as he did, neon blue sparks started to race and crackle through his body. Of all the pieces he could have played, he dived right into the piece I was reluctant to attempt; one of Paganini's twenty-four Caprices. And it was wonderful.

He opened his eyes, staring straight at me and the piece began to grow and get more elaborate, his eyes dancing as he played with supreme skill, finally finishing with a flourish and guiding the instrument to a mournful stop. I'll make it very clear to the reader here, that I have in no way, shape or form felt anything like love for another human male, my brother and father included. Call it a man-crush if you want, but what I felt for Dorian at this moment was awe, respect, admiration and yes, I'll say it, love. Everything that every man could wish to be, was in him, was him and for all the world, I wanted it to be me. For now, though I would have to concede defeat and accept whatever I thought I possessed in terms of breeding, style and taste, on a mountain where I thought I could climb no higher, I found myself a novice, floundering at its feet and basecamp still in the distance.

Dorian finished the piece and moved away from the instrument. He walked over to small, triangle glass table bordered by three sturdy looking chairs, seated himself at one and motioned me to take a seat.

"Be the change you seek, Sherlock," he said. "You say that in order to manipulate space/time, one would have to travel as fast as, if not faster than the speed of light...am I correct?"

I took a seat at the table. "That's what they say."

He folded his hands on the table and smiled at me. "So, what's the answer? I'll give you a clue, I've just told you the answer."

"To be the change I seek."

He smiled again. "SOOO...what's the answer?"

"To become."

"Become what?"

"Become light."

"Eccola, bravo, Sherlock...energy is light, vibration is sound...and every thought and emotion has a number, a color and a sound. Do you dream, Sherlock?"

I nodded vigorously. "Yes."

"And do you dream in color?"

"Sometimes."

"Well, it's dark outside and your eyes are closed...where's the light coming from?" I stared at him in wonder. Of course. I thought of my initial attempts at gathering groups of seven. "Which is why they weren't part of the puzzle," I said... "how do I become light?"

His eyes flashed. "I'll show you." He put his arms on the side of the chair. "Okay, arms like this," he said, "back straight and legs pressed against the chair." I did as I was told. Dorian promptly stood up.

"You will now notice that you can't move."

I tried to lift my arms, but I couldn't, same thing with my legs. I could move my neck and head and wiggle my feet, but that was it. Blind panic began to surge through me.

Dorian approached me and crouched down at my feet.

"At all points of contact, you have become the chair and vice versa. The physical part of the test is over, Sherlock. The final pieces of the puzzle must come from you...from inside you. As above, so below. The only person that can free you from the chair is you, but I'm afraid that you don't have much time."

He thought for a second and then he said, "I'm going to let you into a little secret." With this he retook his seat and breathed deeply. "Please close your eyes," he said.

I did so and was met with an image of the inner workings of a human body. I heard Dorian's voice come in over the top, not through my ears, but from inside my head. "The secret... from the word secretion. The oils, or secretions are Cerebrospinal fluids, and they perform much like an aquifer. They gather in the third ventricle of the brain. One is made by the pituitary gland and one by the pineal gland, one electrical, one magnetic, one white, one yellow, the land of milk and honey...

and they carry a seed. The seed leaves the claustrum...behind the temples...of Solomon...soul of man...sol of man... sun of man...son of man...travels down the spine and empties into Sodom, the lower regions, where the seed dies, unless you have given up your vices. The Quidditas and the seed now travels back up the spine, or Jacob's ladder. Once it has activated the spinning wheels, or the Chakras, the nerve centers along the spine, it continues its journey upwards...the Vagus nerve lies here at the base of the skull and when it passes this, it forms a cross, is crucified and resurrected, puts intense pressure on the electromagnetic crystals gathered there and switches on the antenna, the receiver, or as you call it, your third eye.

His voice then came in through my ears again. "What is the Greek word to anoint, Sherlock?"

"Christos."

"Exactly. And what do you anoint things with?"

I opened my eyes. Dorian was staring at me.

"Oil," I replied.

"Secretions...it's allegorical, the whole thing. Christ is the light." "And God is in you...I believe you tried to make some white powder gold yourself and you are on the right track. It is true that it will activate your pineal gland. But then it has to be harmonized."

With that he went to his side unit and with his back to me, removed something from a drawer.

"The human body doesn't put things in it that it doesn't need, Sherlock, especially in the middle of the brain. Know what this is?" he said turning to me and holding up a tuning fork.

I couldn't lie. "It's a tuning fork!"

"And what is it for?"

"It's an acoustic resonator, that...."

Before I could finish, he struck a crystal on the table with it, placed his left hand firmly on my forehead and slowly began to push the tuning fork up my nose. The feel of the cold steel in my nostrils gave way to discomfort, which in turn became total panic. Tears began to stream down my cheeks, until I could barely make out my tormentor right in front of me. I let out a strangled gasp, as the pain seared through my face.

"We all have a demented sibling hidden away somewhere Sherlock. Would you like to meet mine?"

CHAPTER TWELVE

CHANGELING

He slowly pulled the tuning fork from my nose and at once the pain subsided. I blinked the remaining tears from my eyes, just in time to see Dorian transform before them.

My earlier musings on the horror of waking up tied to a chair in the basement of a serial killer hadn't troubled my mind as much as I thought they would. True, I was sitting on that particular item of furniture and was evidently going nowhere any time soon. True again that I also found myself, though not in a basement of any description, seated only inches above the dungeon where I had watched unspeakable horrors unfold at the hands of my captor.

To my surprise, I remained philosophical about the whole situation, though any outward stoicism I might have exhibited both in my general demeanor and my brash words here, were replaced with a horror more terrifying than any Dorian could inflict on me. I went cold when I realized that sometime soon, with a trillion percent certainty, that I would need to use the bathroom and that in order to avoid an embarrassment worse than any I could suffer at his hands, I would need to solve the next part of the puzzle before I embarrassed myself further still. I needn't have worried, though what then unfurled in front of me in the next sixty seconds would have emptied the bowels of stronger men than me on the spot.

My eyes fixed on Dorian as he started to change. His eyes sparkled ice blue and then glowed red, his benign smile became a twisted snarl and then changed back again, the surface of his skin started to bubble from underneath and he began to grow. I turned my head skywards, as far as my position would allow, but even with my eyeballs straining at the roof of their sockets I couldn't see the top of him. Sharp fingers of fire flickered through him and then were doused with a hiss by heavy threads of neon blue. A pair of black wings five feet wide and again edged in flame, began to unfurl from the main body, but were extinguished almost immediately and replaced with wings of brilliant white and electric blue. Each of the figures were accompanied by a frequency so deep, I could feel it in my bowels...not at all what I needed given the circumstance. The timbre and cadence in the sound changed too, the vibration in each getting faster and louder, creating a feeling of pure disharmony, until the cacophony became unbearable and peaked with a furious interplay between glacier and magma, in what was obviously an argument between an angel of love and creation and one of hatred and destruction. Thankfully the noise then began to recede and as I continued to watch, the process went into reverse, until my enigmatic host stood quietly before me again with a slight look of embarrassment on his face.

"Sorry about that," he said. "A bit of a disagreement there. We rarely see eye to eye. I have a visitor, so I must leave you for a while, but I'm sure you have things to do. And please don't worry, the natural order of things have been suspended in your favor. One less thing to worry about. Hopefully you can join us for the main course, unless you are unsuccessful of course, in which case you will be the main course."

He turned on his heel and strode away. The first thought that came to mind was that if I survived this case, then I would have one hell of a story to tell. Forget Ali v Frazier, forget Alien v Predator. I had just witnessed a fight not just between two brothers, but between two Gods. That story would take all of my powers of conviction and would furthermore depend on whether there were any people left to tell. I had to get out of this situation, and quickly. There wasn't any point looking around the room for something sharp to cut myself free, but I did so anyway. I didn't feel stuck in any sense of the word, what I did feel was that I was partially made of wood. The front half of my body felt human, but gradually lost all feeling towards the back, until I seemed to be and literally was, to all intents and purposes, the chair. The only answer I could come up with was one that anyone in any dangerous situation would do, when all means of escape had been exhausted and all hope was about to follow, just as I had seen in two of Dorian's captives with my own eyes.

I should pray...but to who? I couldn't pray to any God, as being a theosophist, I agreed in the existence of the word, though not in the sense of an all-seeing, celestial dictator, but as a mystical concept, a divine equation, whose secret could only be revealed to the initiated adept. The God inside us all... the God in me. Two hundred years ago, clemency had come at a cost, redemption could be bought from the church, you could actually buy forgiveness and came with the delightful misconception that you could quite literally pray your enemies to death.

Though half of me never saw half of Dorian as an enemy, the other half of me was under no illusion that the other half of him would turn me into pate without batting an eyelid. I knew that the tools I needed were to be found inside me. My plan was to focus on the pulse in my stomach, that was the key I believed. Hopefully the frequency from the tuning fork had harmonized with the monatomic gold and had squeezed my crystals and activated my pineal gland. Maybe this was the route back into my mind palace, so I could at least finish my list and put the puzzle back together in my head.

I remembered what Dorian had said about being able to see better with eyes closed, so after saying a brief prayer to myself and taking a deep breath, I closed them and began to change my frequency. I inhaled what air I could comfortably and then slowly let it out. I contracted whatever organ it was to start the pulse and immediately had the sensation that the bottom of my spine had fallen out, a queasy jump in the pit of the stomach that you get when the floor is suddenly taken from beneath you, or that flash of panic you get when walking alone at night and a car passes you, stops and the reverse lights come on.

The pulse was nearly two seconds long and when I let it go, that familiar warmth began to flush throughout my whole body, emanating from the exact spot from where before there was no feeling at all. Then whoosh, it rose like a coiled serpent up my spine, down my arms and legs together, up through my solar plexus, stomach and chest and barreled up my neck and throat. As I opened my mouth to give the surge an outlet, I felt a rush of air into my head, as if it had been given an extra strong mint and though I couldn't taste it in my mouth, I could taste it in my forehead and as I pondered on the sensation, I felt something being pulled from me, not just something but everything.

It happened so quickly and was so incongruous with the feelings before it, that the only word I could conjure up to describe it, was that whatever it was that I was missing, it seemed like it had been snatched.

Less than half a second later, I was staring down at myself, rooted to the chair, face turned to the sky and mouth wide open. Neon blue light flickered and flashed through my body and seemed to branch out and follow the veins within me. The branches all seemed to converge on the heart and then shot straight up in a shimmering shaft of unbroken light, then broke off into two, one half lighting up the top of my head and the other pouring from my throat. I then made what I thought would be a huge mistake but needn't have worried. I tried not to but just couldn't resist it.

I opened my eyes. I was back in the chair with the table in front of me and again facing the door. I looked down at my body, but there were no lights shooting through me. I caught the sight of myself in a cabinet's glass door, and everything was as it should be. My head wasn't blue and neither was my throat and it would serve me right if when I closed them again, they didn't come back and never would.

Had I spoiled everything already? I imagined that I was back in my dingy little flat next to the river. I took another deep breath, closed my eyes and there I was...back in my shit-hole. I was standing across the street from my humble dwelling. I looked left and right up and down the street, and everything was there.

There was a breeze blowing up the street and on it came the smell of oil and bricks and rotting wood and off in the distance I could hear the snarl of the traffic. I looked up at the window that I spent a lot of time looking down from and saw through the curtainless glass, the vast wall away to the left, covered with my lists. I quickly came to the realization that I was what people call remote viewing and that while I could be there, I couldn't move around, I could only observe. At the same time, I also deduced that, much like Schrödinger's cat, therein lay the answer to not seeing any lights shooting through my body when I opened my eyes. The difference was whether or not something was being observed. I decided that the need to know something was happening was far stronger than the need to see it happening.

Where could I go? Could I be anywhere I chose? Could I only observe? How could I affect change? How could consciousness alter matter?

What I really needed to do was to get myself upstairs with my lists in front of me and put this damn puzzle back together, but before I could do that I needed to see where I was up to with it. Dorian had a visitor...who was it? If it was Elli-Mae Price, then I needed to find victim number six, but if it wasn't our favorite politician, then number six was probably the guest, and it was her I had to find. It would also mean that I was almost out of time.

I opened my eyes and was once more tied to the chair. I waited and I listened, but apart from the delicate strains of the wandering harp, the house was silent. After making a quick scan of my body, I reset myself, closed my eyes, took my breaths and began the sequence once again. The strength of the pulse surprised me, though as the feeling of the Quidditas started to spread through my body, the surge up my spine and the back of my neck felt more powerful. The minty clearing in my head opened up wide and I felt that my cerebrospinal fluid was pouring into the gap and as it reached the base of my skull, I felt the crystals being squeezed and my receiver flickered on.

First things first, I needed to know who the guest was. If I couldn't move around the house freely, then I guessed that I needed to know the layout of the place I wished to go and to do that, I needed to have been there before, which narrowed the choices down. So, I picked the kitchen. I brought to mind the chrome and marble surfaces, the cooker and fridge and the table laden with wine and cheese.

The pulse in my solar plexus was stronger still, the resulting surge sharper and more defined, like it knew what to do and within a few seconds I was standing in the kitchen watching Lyra the barmaid from the Diogenes handing a drink to victim number six. At that moment Dorian entered the kitchen and extended his hand towards his guest.

"Thomas!" he exclaimed, "good to see you again, so glad you could make it. I trust you came alone? No driver, no PR people, no girls, no lawyer."

Thomas laughed as he accepted Dorian's hand. "I know, right? I think it's two years since I drove a car and more than that since I travelled anywhere alone. Took me a minute to find." He looked around. "And here you are, living in a ...what the hell is it, some kind of pyramid house. It's like Ancient Egypt in this motherfucker. Am I the first here?"

"Jameson's, one cube of ice," Lyra said. Thomas drained the glass instantly and handed it back to her. She looked at him for a second. "I'll get you another."

He jerked his head in the direction of the departing Lyra. "And who's she?.... Is it a she?" Dorian smiled benignly at his guest. "My assistant, Lyra. She is now. I allow him to be herself."

Thomas sneered. "I'm full of coke, I don't really mind."

He sidled up to Dorian in a more confidential manner. "Is he here?"

Dorian looked puzzled. "Is who here?"

Thomas's face dropped. "When I accepted the invitation, you promised us a delicacy without equal. I am only here on the strict understanding that he would be here. Don't tell me that I've dropped a million and come all the way out here and he's not even...."

Before he could finish however, Dorian put a finger to his lips and stared intently at him. He then projected an image to Thomas. I know he did this, because the same image was projected to me and it frightened the very life out of me. The image he had projected was of me stuck to the chair.

Thomas relaxed and smiled at Dorian, who in turn looked over and smiled directly at me. My spine fell out. Could he see me? But I wasn't there. Well, my spirit or my consciousness was, but my physical body wasn't. Whether I was visible to my benevolent host or not was supremely beside the point. The point being that I had no time to lose. I had to get out of there, and I had to do so before the cocaine wore off and the guests got hungry.

Though the subject had been previously treated with levity and mirth, it wasn't so funny when the reality of it hit me. Dorian had invited people to his house for a dinner party, and they were without a doubt turning up in all their finery tonight with the sole intention of eating the brain of Sherlock Holmes.

As my mind struggled to shake this terrible image, I was hit by another of my epiphanitos. Oil! When I was standing on my street in the dark just now, I was able to smell and hear! How? I thought that I could only observe. If I could smell, see and hear, could I also taste and touch? Could I move? I closed my eyes and smiled in anticipation, as my body began the familiar process of generating the pulse.

I was right back on the street and stood exactly where I expected to be. I could still smell the oil and could still hear the traffic. If I could possibly have taken a deep breath within a deep breath, then that's what I did and then off I went, walking across the street. I took the keys from my front trouser pocket, then felt my hand extend in front of me as I

approached the door. I saw my hand with the key in it, saw the shape of the key, saw the door, saw the lock...and then I watched in utter amazement as my hand went right through it and disappeared up to the wrist. I pulled my hand back in panic, expecting to see a bloody stump, but back it came in one piece.

I transferred the keys to my other hand and held the original up in front of my face and wiggled my fingers, then cautiously extended my hand again and watched it reach right through the door and was gone again. To say I felt no resistance would be a lie, though I never felt it with the outside of my skin, where things we pick up, or hold, or touch are usually felt. I felt the resistance inside my hand and even then, not resistance as I understood it. My hand felt like it was being pulled from one side of the inside and pushed from the other. I felt the transference of the atoms and gave myself wholly to that not unpleasant feeling. I pushed my arm in up to the shoulder, then quickly withdrew it, put the keys back in my pocket and with a deep breath and my hands extended in front of me, I walked right through the front door and into the hallway.

I stood still for a second and then looked back at the door and then back at myself, again holding out my arms and legs for a quick count. All was well. Foolishly I reached up to make sure my head was still there...it was and at the same time it wasn't, as my hand went right through it. I walked towards the rickety staircase and paused, unsure as to whether the steps would hold my feet, or would I just walk through the staircase? They held and I climbed them carefully. Halfway up, I turned to look over the balcony at the door to the room I was headed, for the very good reason that there were voices coming from it. Who the hell was in my flat? Rightly indignant and with no mind for resistance, I reached the top of the stairs, strode quickly along the landing and straight through the door and into the living room.

Doctor Watson was sitting on a chair facing the main wall, with a look of confusion and exasperation. My insidious brother, Mycroft, was standing over him and was also fixated with the contents of the wall. Two men in black, without question my brother's henchmen and most shockingly in the corner, sitting on the floor and nursing a foot that was covered in blood, was Inspector Lestrade. What on Earth was going on? The question was rhetorical as it was quite obvious what was happening. I had gotten out just in time. My flat had been compromised and my whereabouts had been discovered, though not my current one.

Grace's phone had done some of the damage when she had arrived the day before, though I had thrown them off the scent by sending the phone to the other side of the bridge with the urchins. I deduced that Dr. Watson had seen Grace in town, probably boarding her bus home and with a bit of good old detective work on the only rain-free day this week, had followed the trail of grape juice that had leaked from the bus stop, back through the miserable streets and all the way to my front door. Dr. Watson in turn was easy to find as he wasn't trying to hide. He in turn had called the inspector and was then himself easily tracked by Mycroft and his goons, who, if I had got this right, were holding Dr. Watson at gunpoint and forcing my poor friend to reveal the secrets on the wall.

Fury erupted inside me. Forty-five years of sibling rivalry came to a sudden head, and I launched myself at Mycroft, as he stood menacingly over the good doctor. Tyson-like, I jumped into the punch and would have separated his head from his shoulders, had my fist not sailed cleanly through it and sent me sprawling across the floor. I lay there staring up at Dr. Watson as he struggled in the chair. I sprung to my feet and tried a couple of left jabs, followed by a right cross, then another left jab, followed by a straight right, then just for good measure I wound up a haymaker and let him have it, which ended up with me on the floor again. Though I never touched him once, it felt amazing and I lay on the floor laughing hysterically. In time I calmed down and focused on Dr. Watson.

"As I see it," he stumbled, "it's all based around the number seven. Here we have seven planets and seven parts of the body. Over here, we have seven wonders of the world."

Mycroft cast a doubting look at the doctor. "Easter Island isn't a wonder of the world," he said.

Dr. Watson looked over at that particular list. "I know. Easter Island isn't on the list." Mycroft was getting impatient.

"Rapa Nui IS Easter Island," he snapped.

Dr. Watson tried to think on the spot. "Quite so," he agreed. "Then we have..."

"Dr. Watson, you have absolutely no idea what you are talking about, have you?" The doctor squirmed uncomfortably in his chair but held on to himself. He was quite offended. "Give me a minute," he retorted, "it normally takes me a little while to zone in."

I stared at my hands and then jumped back to my feet. I couldn't affect change from here. I needed to be inside his head and in order to do so, I needed to get back to my own chair. I opened my eyes and was back in Dorian's house directly.

I focused on my good friend, valiantly trying to solve my puzzle. I thought of his gentle nature, of his forgiving and ready smile. I thought of his simple head and its well-meaning harmless contents. The minty space in my head began to open. Suddenly there was a flash, and I saw the wall of lists before me. It flickered and then came back with more clarity and better color. It flashed again and I was able to hold the image for a few seconds. I scanned the lists and found I was able to navigate them with relative ease. Letters started to jump out at me from the wall. Patterns began to form and it seemed for all the world that my powers were starting to come back. I also had audio! I knew this because the vision I held in my head froze for a second, the image shifted down to the floor, as if in secrecy, and then I heard the soft, excited though hushed tone of Dr. Watson in my head.

"Holmes?"

Boom! I'm in! Right, first I needed to see what Dorian

and Lyra were up to and then I could concentrate on the problem by the river. I closed my eyes and went through my routine. I found myself in the kitchen again, though standing in the doorway, between rooms. Off to the left was a living room I hadn't been in yet but could see from where I stood that Dorian was sitting on a sofa with his back to me. He was watching some kind of reportage on a large screen. On the right of me was the kitchen. Lyra had just entered and was furnishing the latest guest with another drink.

I inched into the living room first and turned my eyes towards the screen. Dorian was sitting on the end of a large sofa with his legs folded underneath him, entranced by the presenter on the screen. I guessed that he knew I was standing behind him, but he made no indication that he was aware of my presence and continued to watch. The program was a 60-minute special from Australia and judging by the presenter's suit, her school clothes and the furniture, it looked like the piece was shot in the early eighties. The male presenter was interviewing a young girl of maybe twelve or thirteen years of age from London. I had no idea on the nature of the content of the show, but the interview unfolded thus.

"And how many men were you forced to have sex with?"

CHAPTER THIRTEEN

THE REMEMBERING

The young girl gazed at the floor between them; her eyes held no spark of life whatsoever.

"Depends how many were there," she said. "Twenty, sometimes thirty."

"And you were handed around by these men. Under whose orders? Who was supposed to be looking after you."

"My gran."

"Your grandma? With your mum absent, she was the one person in the world you should trust to keep you safe. And what was she doing while these men were abusing you."

"She was laughing. Or having sex herself...with other men."

"And were these normal people, like you and me?"

"No, they were posh. Very posh. We were always taken somewhere. Normally to a big house with gates, like a castle."

"And would you recognize this big house, if you saw it again?"

"Yes, but I have no idea how to get there. We were blindfolded and drugged on the way."

A groan came from Dorian. Lyra entered and handed a

glass to him. He looked haunted. He turned back to the screen and as Lyra left the room again, I followed her into the kitchen. Tom was looking around the place. He turned to Lyra as she entered the kitchen.

"And will you be taking part in tonight's proceedings?"

Lyra stood with her hands clasped behind her back, watching him. "I'll be here," she said.

Tom walked slowly towards her, sinking his drink as he did so. "And what's your story? I mean you're a man right?"

He took another step and then stopped, put his hand out to the wall and shook his head. He looked at his empty glass and then it fell from his grasp. Lyra opened a cupboard and retrieved a broom. She addressed the guest matter-of-factly, as she cleared up the glass around him. He wobbled where he stood and continued to try and shake some sense back into his head.

"My story is simple really," she said. "I am a biological male, born into a life of constant violent, sexual assault and degradation. So much so that by the age of twelve I had subconsciously developed an alter ego. One that was tough, one that was confident. One who couldn't be hurt anymore."

Tom sank to his knees on the kitchen floor. Lyra crouched beside him and put her head close to his. "By people like you!" she hissed.

Tom collapsed in a heap. Lyra smiled as she looked down at him.

I jolted in my chair; I had no time to lose. Number six was about to die and though number five was still swanning about at liberty somewhere, the game was hurtling towards its conclusion, and I was as far from solving it as I ever was. I reset myself and began the sequence to get back into Dr. Watson's head. I looked up at the lists, and they finally began to dance. I saw immediately how everything was to link up. I saw the geometrical shapes, the Sumerian Gods, the numbers, the angles, the letters, the fractals and the quanta that divided it and kept it all together. Everything was crystal clear and though I wasn't totally back in my mind palace, I did feel the familiar energy that accompanied it. Dr. Watson then burst into life and I heard him say.

"These clusters of circles here represent the cell structure of everything, living or otherwise. They represent precisely the seed of life and here on a bigger scale, the flower of life."

Dr. Watson stood and moved across to the world map. "The Torus energy of planet Earth has given us the energy lines on which an object, once it has reached the desired frequency, can travel easily between dimensions."

I felt Dr. Watson pause and my vision shifted to the floor, again as if in secrecy. I focused everything on trying to intimate to the good doctor to not look so suspicious, as my brother would pick that up immediately. I was too late, however. The images flickered, fizzed and then disappeared. I was no longer inside the mind of Dr. Watson but was remote viewing once more. My brother had turned from the wall and was sending a text on his phone.

"Thank you, Dr. Watson," he said, "that will do for now." He jabbed a thumb at Inspector Lestrade, who was still clinging to his foot in the corner. "I believe that he would benefit from your medical expertise for a while."

Dr Watson, though rather pained, as he was just getting into his groove, gratefully left the puzzle, grabbed his bag and crouched by the inspector, who was starting to slip in and out of consciousness. "Shit!" I thought. The link was broken again, and I was relegated to the point of observer once more.

He retrieved a syringe and bottle from the bag and began to prepare something for the man's pain. There was a knock at the door and one of Mycroft's goons went to answer it. It was another of his henchmen, who entered carrying a silver aluminum case, which he set on the floor and began to empty its contents onto the table. Inspector Lestrade gave a loud sigh, as Dr. Watson gave him his shot of morphine. He put his hand behind the inspector's head and gently lay it down, with a towel beneath it. The doctor sat back on his haunches and sighed heavily. I went back to check on Dorian.

Dorian was seated where I had left him, though now had a bottle of wine in front of him and was getting visibly more upset. On screen, the interviewer was still with Theresa. "Sometimes, they would just get homeless people off the street and kill them. But they weren't eaten, they were just killed."

Away to the right of the room, sat a bank of monitors. On one of the smaller screens, I saw Lyra dragging an unconscious Tom by one foot down the corridor. On another screen, I saw myself stuck to the chair. With a stab of pride, I saw that I was not at all panicked by my predicament. I watched myself sitting calmly, eyes closed and fingers of electricity streaking throughout my body. On a large screen in the center, the exploded Metatron cube slowly spun. To my mixture of horror and delight, I saw that the puzzle was nearly complete. I counted quickly that there were only fourteen circles left and the rest of the puzzle span beautifully in the middle. That must mean that the megalithic sites and the Sumerian Gods were correct guesses, though Dorian had said that strictly speaking there were no right or wrong answers and my offering of gifts that those Gods had given to the human race were also correct. "What we gave you. What you took. You can see what's missing, if you dare to look."

I racked my brains.... What's missing? From where? Dare to look? Dare to look where? Was there something missing from the victims? It looked to me like I had two clues to solve and two victims to save, three if you counted Tom, but as I watched him being dragged down the corridor and out of shot, I didn't. I opened my eyes and was back stuck to my chair. A few minutes later the door opened and Lyra appeared pushing Tom in a wheelchair. He was gagged and gaffer taped to the chair. His eyes bulged in his head as Lyra deposited him at the table facing me, then turned and left the room, closing the door behind her.

I was running out of time. Ignoring the petrified sod in front of me, I closed my eyes, reset myself and took myself back to the Watsons head. After a few flickers, the connection was made and once more the wall, resplendent with its lists, lay again before me. I could feel something wasn't right though. There seemed to be an extra hum coming from somewhere. It wasn't interference but was most certainly resistance and we were losing energy somewhere. I figured that could only mean one thing, and right then I didn't have time to check, but it gave me an idea. My focus was entirely on the lists in front of me. My old methods began to ooze back through my pores again and, as I looked, things came fast and easy, just as they had always done. In bright, colorful flashes I saw the megalithic temples again, the Sumerian Gods, star systems and geometric patterns. Letters started to jump out and were highlighted as they did. Dr. Watson got to his feet, grabbed a marker and started to write on the wall, explaining to Mycroft as he went.

"It's in the letters...in the names," he/we said, "elementary my dear Mycroft. Just need to look for patterns. We have the victims so far. Montague Frobisher, Rosalind Parker, Michael O'Driscoll, Harry Adler, Ella-Mae Price, who was taken first and then escaped.

Take the initials, MF, RP, MOD, HA and EMP. Rosalind Parker and Harry Adler were taken together, so that would be MF, MOD, HARP and EMP."

Mycroft had already spotted the pattern and had moved close to the wall with renewed excitement. He pulled his phone from his pocket and sent a text. Dr. Watson was gaining in confidence and began to discover his touch. He/I continued.

"Sherlock advises me that there are no such things as coincidences, but if we look over here, we find F432 written here and a line drawn all the way out up to Alaska. After careful study of the problem, I think you'll find that the names are all acronyms. So, we have, I believe, Magnetic Field, Electro-Magnetic Pulse Weapons, Ministry of Defense and the High-frequency Active Aural Project, which if my mind serves me correctly, is to be found...."

Before he could finish, I jumped from inside Dr. Watson's head and continued to watch from the doorway. One of Mycroft's goons had typed something into his phone. Mycroft turned to him expectantly. The goon read from the screen.

"Alaska Airlines. Flight 432 to Anchorage. Twice a day."

Without another word, Mycroft and his mob made for the door and disappeared as quickly as they had arrived. I turned from the wall and looked at my friend Dr. Watson, who had sat back down and was removing circular sticking pads from his head. That's where we were losing energy. Mycroft had obviously become suspicious of Dr. Watson's abilities and had evidently tried to tap in to his and my brain waves and in doing so, had unwittingly and somewhat predictably walked right into my trap.

I left Dr. Watson to tend to the distraught inspector by opening my eyes and as expected found myself once more in my physical realm, again static, but this time with company. I stared at the man in front of me, who had calmed down somewhat and was actively taking stock of his situation. Had he not been gagged, he could have asked me what I thought lay in store for us both and though in reality our predicaments differed wildly, I felt I was ready to comment on his current plight. Sometime before my incapacity, I deduced that the occupation of the victims was linked to a chakra and somehow foretold of the manner of their execution. The banker being figuratively the arse-end of society, was found with a shattered coccyx, the priest was found with his guts gone, Harry Adler had had his internal organs removed prior to being cooked and our judge Rosalind Price I expect was eaten by Dorian minus the black muscle that beat feebly in her chest. All manners of death, all chakras, all missing. Root gone, sacral gone, solar plexus gone, heart gone. That was the physical chakras below the heart taken care of, I had three to go, which would be mental, spiritual, ethereal or astral. With Ellie-Mae Price still free to roam for the time being at least, I guessed that the man who sat in front of me right now, used his throat for a living and was in all probability going to be missing it soon. I looked deep into his eyes and asked the question that I now knew the answer to.

"I gather you're a singer," I said.

The man nodded and for a second there was a flicker of hope in his eyes, though that dissipated immediately with the realization that, not only was his fame not going to get him out of this, but even if it could, it wouldn't, as I had no idea who the hell he was, which that very premise hinged on. I did know one thing however and I told him straight.

"I don't think this is going to go well for either of us," I said.

Secretly I rather hoped that it would go much worse for him than it ever would for me and had seven very good reasons for thinking that way. What had I done? The worst thing I could be accused of would be failing a test...hardly a death sentence, though I had accepted the challenge, knew the risks, but still privately held the belief that when it came to disposing of me, that my death would be somewhat dignified given the scope and integrity of the task ahead. I didn't mind one bit that my brain was going to be eaten, just spare me the fire, spare me the medieval torture devices, spare me the humiliation of wetting myself and spare me the pain. That was all down to Dorian and the mood he was in. The mood that they were in. I thought I'd better go check on them. As I stared into the last few minutes of life in this man's eyes, I started the pulse and waited and as I did so, I reflected on the delicious factoid that the person who held me captive, was indeed two different brothers and the human being they occupied, so was three individual entities and still didn't have the gall to introduce themselves in the plural. Wondering how those so unsighted could call themselves woke, I closed my eyes.

Dorian's mood had changed and as he sat on the sofa drinking wine, I could feel a bend in the force. On screen the interviewer was almost too shocked to ask Theresa any more questions. He sighed and tried to gather himself, Theresa still stared at nothing. He pushed on.

"You say that the homeless people were just killed. What do you mean by *just* killed?"

Theresa breathed out heavily and then looked at the presenter.

"They didn't eat the homeless, they only ate the babies."

"And where did they get the babies from?"

"They would breed them. Also, babies without documentation, or they would pay the parents to have them. I had four children of my own. Only one survived, for about an hour. Then she died."

"And what did they do with them then? The stillborn and the ones that died."

"They made me eat them."

A mournful howl rose from deep within Dorian. He threw his glass at the screen and stood up from the sofa. At once I knew what was happening and as I looked on in amazement, he began to change. As he did, I saw briefly the Good v

Evil show, but quickly it was bad Dorian all the way. He wrenched himself away from the main body and grew in fantastic and horrible isolation. His skin bubbled, turned black and turned to scales. His arms stretched out and from them his fiery wings unfurled and then shook themselves alight. At that moment Lyra entered the room and watched with pride as Dorian transformed in front of us both. She stood by my side and though she could not see me, when a tearful good Dorian dropped with exhaustion back onto the sofa, he turned his head and with his heart completely broken addressed us both.

"They made her eat her own baby," he said.

My attention, however, was fixed solely on Enlil, as he reached the point of transformation. Seething with orange and red and shot through with spark and flame, he stood tall unfurled his wings and produced the most unearthly, ear-splitting scream I would ever experience. He then shrunk quickly back into the size of a man, his outer shell being flayed from him before my eyes, till stood before me was a snarling, spitting, seething version of the man on the sofa. Before me, I beheld bad Dorian.

He turned to the bank of screens and focused on the only one that was active. The one with me and the singer stuck to the chairs. He turned and looked at us both and made for the doorway and though I could see myself on the screen, I knew that I wasn't really there but needed to be. I closed my eyes and opened them stuck to the chair. Tom continued to stare at me with resignation and sadness and as I looked into his eyes, I wondered the question, the same one I had asked of all the victims.

"What did you do?"

I already knew the answer, so the question I didn't need to voice, the thought of the question alone sent images and sounds firing through my head. The sounds of screams, not just any screams, screams of children...I saw tears and felt the horror of what the man in front of me had done. I was there, I knew what he had done and I didn't want to see any more. I wanted him to suffer the same fate, the same way, with the same pain, the same fright, the exact same loss of hope and the excitement that now overtook me was in the knowledge that the creature who we could now hear storming down the hallway, thought exactly the same way as I did.

I smiled sadly at Tom, and he stared back at me through wasted tears, that now, ironically fell freely down his face. Whoever the tears were for they were too late now. He threw a last despairing look at the door before it exploded inwards in a storm of shards and splinters, leaving the image of the arbiter of revenge and retribution simmering in the doorway.

Tom let out an involuntary squeal and immediately pissed himself, as he took in the forbidding sight of his executioner, whose eyes were drilling a hole in the singer's head.

Dorian took a small step towards the singer, reached out and closed his fingers around the singer's throat. With no effort whatsoever, the grip tightened and he started to lift the captive into the air, chair and all. Tom's eyes strained at their sockets, as the pressure built and the blood started to fill up his face.

"There comes a time in every man's life, where he is called to account for his actions," he said. He held the singer out at arm's length, looking him straight in his eyes, that were now starting to fill up with blood.

Lyra now appeared in the doorway and without acknowledging my presence, folded her arms and watched on with mild amusement. "And he will stand in the hall of judgement, and his life will be measured."

Dorian seemed to be working himself into a frenzy, as he spoke his words served to darken his mood and his temper rose accordingly.

"And he will not leave until a balance has been struck, until he has faced his crimes and atoned for his sins."

As I watched on in terrified admiration, Dorian's fingernails broke the skin of the singer and began to push on through his throat. His voice grew in volume and in anger. "Sometimes, the sins are so great and the crimes so many, that a balance cannot be struck. Sometimes the character of a person is so far from help that there can be no forgiveness, there can be no redemption. But for them, even death holds no escape and for me, that's when the fun really begins."

He pulled the singer close to him, looked into Tom's frantic eyes and smiled. "I'll be waiting for you," he said.

With that he closed his fist. There was a loud sucking sound, as the last breath was taken from him, a quick jolt and Dorian pulled the singer's windpipe from his throat. The chair dropped and the flap of skin that used to be the singer's neck fell back, leaving the opening of his throat exposed and his head staring wildly down his own back. Dorian squeezed the rest of the flesh through his fingers and then wiped his hand on the singer's jacket. As he turned to leave, he glanced at me briefly and smiled.

"And hopefully you'll be waiting for me."

As he left the room, he stopped and addressed Lyra, who watching on with her arms behind her back.

"You can have the next one, I promise," he said.

With that he was gone and I realized that I was shaking. Maybe I had become complacent. If I thought for one second that I was somehow teacher's pet and that I would get preferential treatment, I was sadly mistaken. Panic began to rise within me. I had to get the fuck out of here and I had to do it now. I strained at the chair that held me in its invisible grip. I tried to stay calm, but I wanted to cry and scream and fight all comers, and this wasn't the way to do it. I knew how to do it; I was right all along. One thing and one thing only would allow me to escape this chair and get me back into my mind palace. For it to happen though, I needed Dr. Watson and I needed him here now. If my great friend wanted me to solve this puzzle, escape and the human race to survive, he would have to do what I asked of him. I knew in my very bones that he wasn't going to like it and would very probably say no. Before getting back into the doctor's head though, I needed to see how the land lay with Dorian, as the scene I had just witnessed gave me every indication that the tables had turned against me.

Enlil was raging and looked like he wasn't about to be stopped. If anything it felt like things had speeded up, gotten more serious and that the end for me and indeed for everyone else would come much sooner than expected. I needed to find Elli-Mae Price before Dorian did, but I couldn't do that in my current state. I started the process to turn on my receiver. By my deduction I was a clue behind. I had five victims but had only solved four parts of the puzzle so far. I didn't worry about it though, as I was quite confident that I knew what the next one was.

With my receiver flashing like a beacon, I imagined again that I was in the doorway, between the kitchen and the lounge, a room I had only seen from afar. With my heart banging in my chest, I appeared there and made my way into it. Apart from the bank of screens in the center of the room, the middle one of which showed the swirling insignia nearly complete, I knew nothing of this room. It wasn't dark, but was very low-lit.

The room, though housed in a pyramid, was given a circular aspect due to there being no straight lines or sharp edges. All joins, joints and joists were smooth and picked out in neon blue and gave an overall smooth feel to it. Over to the left of the room was a black leather reclining racing seat, facing the screens and next to this spinning freely in the air to the side of the chair, was a neon blue ball of Torus energy that gently spat out energy, which clung to its sides, travelled up and fed itself from the top. As I contemplated this sight, good Dorian walked wearily in from a side door and without acknowledging me traipsed slowly towards the chair. With a brief glance at the screen, he sighed heavily and lay down on the chair.

From the other side of the room bad Dorian stomped into view. He growled angrily at the sight of his brother, strode across the room and plonked himself down on the chair too.

From my vantage point, I watched them merge, watched as their bodies good and bad, blue and red, ice and fire, lay down together and became one. Dorian then held out his hand and rested it on top of the Torus energy ball and the whole room came alive. Fingers of electricity shot up the walls and gathered at the top of the building, the room began to breathe, to pulse, to beat, to live. The same was happening to Dorian, his body was flushed with waves of neon light, that raced from his feet to his head and as I watched him come alive, he started to disappear. Neon waves chased themselves into his head and with a whoosh he was gone and I was alone.

I opened my eyes, and I was once again on my chair, though my mood had lifted with the anticipation of what might happen next. I composed myself and began the sequence to turn on my receiver. I thought of holding Dr. Watson's phone, of the words I wanted to say and the message I wished him to receive. Could I send him a text? I wasn't sure and there no way to verify it if I was successful, that would only serve to make me more anxious, so I decided to use the method I had previously engaged. Hopefully he was still there.

As the powerful waves surge North in me, I imagined I was back at the river, staring at my lists, but that was no good, I needed to be inside his head. I reset myself again and imagined I was Dr. Watson. He had obviously felt the same thing because when I appeared back at the dwelling, I was staring down at Inspector Lestrade, who lay on the floor in a medicated stupor. Before either of us could break the connection, I concentrated hard on the most important words of my life. There were just five of them. "Get in taxi. Bring O."

Dr. Watson looked up from his patient, looked at the wall and then wildly around the room. Finally, he realized what was happening. He stared at the wall, and I heard him again say, "Holmes?"

I never answered him, nor indeed tried to communicate anything further, those five words should suffice. He started to move quickly around the room, and I couldn't keep up with him, so I opened my eyes, reset myself and went straight back to him, though as an observer. He was on the phone. I waited patiently as he first called an ambulance to the scene and then called a cab. I waited with him until the cab arrived, watched him get in it and then left him to it. I would return in fifteen minutes to see how he was getting along. In the meantime, I readied myself for what I hoped would be my final bout of viewing remotely, but when I tried to return, I forgot that I had never been in the taxi before, so couldn't recreate with enough detail to be there myself, so I tried again but this time to get back into his head.

Almost immediately I found myself hurtling through the countryside in the dark. The taxi driver was rabbiting on about something, and I was staring straight ahead through the windscreen in total silence.

"Where to now?" I heard the driver say. We had reached a four-way crossroads and were sitting at the intersection with the engine idling. He was getting close. "Left here," I heard Dr. Watson say, "and then straight on at the next one." I stayed with them until I felt Dorian's house was close and then I messaged Dr. Watson to stop the car. The driver did so and then looked around them at the bleak, black nothingness of where they were.

He pulled his face. "Are you sure you want to get out here?"

I'm not sure that I picked up what Dr. Watson's reply was, but there was a pause and then I felt that I was stood up tall and the forest was all around me. I smelled the jasmine and knew he was here.

Quietly I slipped away and opened my eyes. When I did, I looked at the shredded neck of the singer sitting before me, I looked down at the point where my body joined the chair and I started to laugh. And laugh and laugh and laugh like my life depended on it. Truth be told, I felt the tide turning in my favor and I began to think that I might actually get out of this alive. I calmed myself and settled down to wait for Dr. Watson.

While I waited, I conducted a brief recap of where I was up to and what I had to do next. Five victims and four sections completed. Megalithic sites I had seven, Planets likewise, Sumerian Gods, Chakras and gifts given by the Gods to humanity, I also had seven of. The sixth part was obviously the occupation of the victims, of which I had six and would soon hazard a guess at the seventh. They all occupied high-flying jobs and scaled up in terms of importance and prestige, like a pyramid and as that shape dictates, the last would be the top, the pinnacle, the most important. What I was missing was a whole section, the final part of the puzzle and so far, I didn't have a clue what it would be. I relaxed and almost smiled. I felt confident and kind of happy.

I went into remote viewing mode and placed myself in the basement where Dorian had dealt with his victims. I stood there calmly and though I couldn't see him just yet, I knew that Dr. Watson was around somewhere. Suddenly I heard a scratching noise coming from behind the circular door, something or rather someone was behind it. Before I had the chance to lose my patience with him, Dr. Watson fell through the door and onto the floor of the basement. He was soaking wet. He jumped to his feet, as if he were about to be attacked. I laughed to myself and watched him take in his surroundings in horror.

I saw him walk past the crystals, past the table that held the tools and on into the elevator. I watched him exit and make his way down the curved corridor and stop at the first door, where he looked in on a perfect rendition of my Baker Street flat in amazement. He was close enough now for me to open my eyes, break the connection and scream his name at the absolute top of my lungs. Finally, he appeared in front of me, wet and breathless. He stared me up and down and then looked in horror at the mangled mess who sat opposite me. He wiped water from his face. I was overjoyed to see him.

"Watson! You're here! Quick...hurry up, we have no time to lose," I said.

The good doctor hurried to my side and made as if to untie me. His hands moved around the chair, and he looked underneath and all around it, before looking at me in surprise. "Holmes, thank goodness you're safe. How am I supposed to get you out of this? I can't seem to...what is it, superglue?"

"I can't release myself until I have completed the puzzle."

"Nearly drowned you know. They don't know who they're dealing with. When I was in Afghanistan..."

I didn't have the time for this. I stared at him. "Watson, I need to get out of here. Did you bring it?"

The doctor looked blankly at me. "Did I bring what? What's all the water about? Tunnel was full of it."

I steadied my breath and gave him as swift an explanation as I could muster, given the circumstance. "It's piezoelectricity. The water is funneled through the limestone, where it puts pressure on the quartz crystals to release electricity. The whole place is made from mica, granite and andesite, transfers electro-magnetic energy and also there is a build-up of CO2 that again puts intense pressure on the crystals. The whole place is a massive battery. Did you bring it?"

"Did I bring what?"

The doctor annoyed the hell out of me sometimes. I didn't want to say the word, but he was going to make me do so.

"Watson. I need to get back into my mind palace. I am stuck to this chair...I am this chair, until I can solve the missing parts of the puzzle. Apparently, the physical test is over and the answers I seek are now inside me. In order to solve the missing parts, I need to go deep into my mind palace and the only way I can get back in, is in your bag." Dr. Watson snorted in derision. He didn't like where I was going with this.

"Holmes, I only brought it because I thought that you might be in pain. I gave some to Lestrade, but he's had his bloody toes blown off. I really can't condone it for recreational purposes. Anyway, if I refuse, what are you going to do?" I immediately lost my temper.

"Watson, it wasn't so long ago, you couldn't wait to stick a fucking needle in me," I snarled. "I shouldn't have to remind you, that I am in this predicament because of you and your virtue-signaling and paranoia. I'm only locked out because you injected me with a substance that made me lose my memory. In the meantime, people have died and if you don't let me back in, then everybody will die...including you." Dr. Watson refused to budge. He laughed. The bastard laughed.

"Oh no, Holmes, you're not getting me like that. That was a genuine mistake and was probably your brother who sent the vaccine to your flat. So don't blame me. I am genuinely sorry for what happened, but I made a promise to myself that I would never force you to have another jab and I for sure won't be giving any to you. I'm afraid you'll have to find another way."

I looked at him sadly. "So, you're just going to let me die again?" I said.

"What do you mean, again?"

When you gave me that bloody vaccine, you didn't kill me on the outside, but inside me that day, everything died."

"Oh, don't be so dramatic. You know I would never intentionally hurt you." As he said these words, he softened and I knew that I had him. "I don't want to do it, Holmes.

Please don't make me do it."

"Believe me, Watson, if there was another way, I would take it immediately. This is my last chance. You are my last chance. You are everybody's last chance."

It worked. Dr. Watson toughened up on the spot. He dived into his bag and fished out his silver case, from which he produced a syringe. His face tightened and I knew he was in a foul mood. He produced a bottle of liquid, plunged the syringe into the top and stopped.

"Holmes," he said, "there must be another way." I readied myself. "There is no other way," I said.

"Holmes, I really don't want to."

"We're wasting valuable time, Watson."

"This is the last time, Holmes," he said. "And when this is done, I am going to leave your services, and you will never see me again."

I was excited and not at all worried that he would leave me. I could talk him round when it was all over. If it ever would be. "Fine," I said, "it's a deal."

The doctor sighed heavily, as he placed the needle over a vein. "I mean it, Holmes," he said, I'll walk away. You'll be dead to me."

I didn't answer him. I closed my eyes and waited for that old familiar sensation to flood my body; I also closed them so that I wouldn't see Dr. Watson crying as he delivered the shot. Neither would I see him, when he turned his back, wiped the needle and returned it to his case. I wouldn't see him wipe the tears from his face with the back of his sleeve and in return for this, he wouldn't need to see the smug look of victory on my face, the insidious drug taking hold of my body and easing it into the Victorian cesspit of my mind, where all my answers lived. Alas he would also not get to witness the fact that right in front of him I had quickly and quietly just passed away.

CHAPTER FOURTEEN

PASCAL'S WAGER

Now I know that my graveside manner can be somewhat agricultural and this had been honed and kept keen recently with my newly implemented regimen and the frequently offered dictum to Dr. Watson and Mrs. Hudson, when railroading me to jump on with theirs and the government's plans to make me better, that to my knowledge there was nothing at all in my body to make me die. That had now all changed...I did now and if the massive dose of heroin that Dr. Watson had just pumped into me hadn't have seen me off, then his poxy vaccine would have done. I smiled at the thought that after all the fuss had died down, I hadn't even been given the vaccine.

How ironic. Whatever, if Dr. Watson hadn't got me with one jab, he'd have got me with another. I was happy that I had managed to retain my sense of humor and as I slipped into familiar territory, I was taken by the spirit of Monty Python again. No, it wasn't my first time, yes, I knew the way...line on the left, one cross each. I was dying but I wasn't sad and I wasn't scared; as always, I would have my choices. Or so I thought

I could renew my contract and return to my original self,

not here in the physical realm, only as consciousness before I became a 2d ribbon of printed information, which would be blasted with light, pop 3d and a human form would start to grow.

I could also stay where I was but be able to communicate with beings in their physical state, like a ghost. This choice initially held some attraction for me, as it played to everyone's favorite superpower of being invisible, though I accept that even this would eventually lose its sparkle, if I should ever need someone to talk to or somebody to touch. Nowadays I would choose radar, sonar, echolocation and bioluminescence over invisibility, though not at the expense of my brain, which is hilarious given that this was the currency being traded in this particular deal.

Admittedly I could return to experience another human life...though being plagued by the tragedy of my current existence, that wasn't very likely; the painful business of being a human being again couldn't be accepted off the bat. Could I choose the situation? Could I choose who and where? I got what I was given this time round and was eternally grateful for it, I suppose. Born into privilege under the impatient tutelage of my industrialist father, who gave me nothing except a taste for the finer things in life and a fear of closeness. If I could choose, I would be a nobody who knew no one, so this choice was a complete waste of time.

I could sit in discussion with those in a similar situation, but we would all have to agree to go to departure to that territory. I dismissed this option out of hand, as to agree on a destination, I would first need to agree on which people to discuss it with and I probably wouldn't do that.

I could assume a physical life as another life at another site, which would put me totally at the mercy of somebody else's decision making and though I profess to not being very fond of human beings, they would still be my preferred choice of life form. True I could come back as a Nordic from Pleiades, an Eben or a Grey, but equally I could find myself a parasite living in a vulture's gut.

I could also study other phases of the consciousness continuum and though I have no clue what this means exactly, I made a guess that it would be much the same as the first choice, existing outside my or any physical body, though would not be the same consciousness which I now experience.

These were my choices. Now each time I had died, I thought I had been given the same set of choices and had made the decision from the start that should the situation present itself again, then I would move along to a different choice and select a different one every time. Naturally I chose the most attractive proposition at the time, and they diminished in terms of appeal the more I died and the more complacent I got. Oh, my learned friend, if I tell you that in this mortal endgame, at which I thought I was a master, that I had made a grave mistake and was potentially facing an eternity as bad as any I could imagine. It was only now, as the void started to swallow me, that I realized that I didn't have any choices left. I had used up six of them in my six deaths...but there was one left, the one that I had avoided from the start at all costs. The one that I would choose behind burning in fire for all of time...walking into the light and joining up with my ancestors.

I couldn't bear the thought of five minutes in a room with my present family and here I was with it as the only option left. This couldn't be happening. I stood and looked at the growing light in confusion. Should I walk towards it? I didn't want to.

I turned around but the universe wasn't laid out before me as usual, the geometric buffet that was on offer was no longer all you can eat, but was now not even a take it or leave it situation. If I died this time, if I truly died, then I would get what I was given and if I didn't eat it now, I would get it for breakfast, this was my destiny and I had chosen it. Now it was mine for eternity.

I turned back, telling myself to not walk into it, but I didn't need to, it was the only option left and it was coming right towards me. I didn't want to die. Not like this. Dying was only an attractive proposition when the choices were still available and as I floated away, lamenting my lack of patience, I went over the choices again, that all now seemed highly attractive. I could be a ghost, I would make a great ghost, or poltergeist. I could drag my chains and remove my head and moan and wail and scream. I would be the gentleman ghost, for the more discerning victim. Ghost to the stars. A ghost to the rich and famous. I wouldn't mind either, all things considered, coming back for another crack at humanity, though not in the same body or knowing the same people. An ironic twist that my reason for not wanting to choose this one off the bat, was for the exact reason I used to eschew the meeting of new people, of more people, as I hadn't spent enough time with the people I already know. I would even sit and chat with others in a similar situation and would democratically go along with the destination chosen as a group. Anything but this and though I hate to say the words that sum up the totality of the intelligence of modern society, this time I had to agree in full with them and could give no better explanation for where I found myself that this time, that it is what it is.

Even with all the times I had been in this situation, I wasn't aware how long I had before the light disappeared, as I had chosen quickly-hastily-every time before. It was no longer coming towards me but stayed at some distance and shadowy figures appeared in the light and began to beckon me to them. I knew I had to start walking towards the light, but I stayed routed to the spot. I didn't know the figures who called me to them, they had no faces, but they gave off an air of benevolence, the invitation felt sincere, but still, I didn't move. If I stayed there, would the light fade and the offer be withdrawn? Would I be trapped in limbo, a more haunted and tortured soul than I already was? And of all the choices I had been given, whatever they were, each one was the next thing, a new form, a new life, a new experience, a new lesson and everyone would get one, apart from me.

So, this was it, was it? I, Sherlock Holmes, the great detective, dead for real? There would be no resurrection party, no scandals in the press as to where I really was, no clothes found on the beach and no further false alarms for Dr. Watson and Mrs. Hudson to suffer. At last, they could grieve for me properly, though there wouldn't be anything left of me to bury. My wish after my death was to have a sky burial; I quite liked the idea of going back to nature this way. Fire was a bit drastic; the terrifying thought of being setting alight while I was dead did not seem any more appealing nor any less horrific to me, than going up in flames while being alive. Being buried in the ground and going back to the Earth I admit does have its appeal, insomuch as I would get to leave a skeleton. I would have something to show to future archaeology as proof I existed and for those who cared about me and loved me, though I suspect the number would be few, somewhere for them to visit and somebody to talk to.

Yes, the thought of going back to nature appealed to me greatly and being an air sign made me think that a sky burial would be my choice. The thought of being swooped away by golden eagles and for whatever was left of me to live on in their offspring was perfect and on a recent trip to Lhasa I was invited to a sky burial by a Yogi friend of mine, which is when I changed my mind. Hovering above me wasn't the majestic, deadly raptors of renown, waiting to carry me away and feast on me. Instead, circling above me, was the scruffy, screeching, hyena of the skies, the bearded vulture. Hundreds of them. To be torn apart and gobbled down without a thought and having my body digested alongside a two-week-old hippo carcass was bad enough, but to see the preparation that went into it, shocked me to my core.

After the corpse was unwrapped, five or six men approached it with heavy clubs, where they proceeded to smash the poor thing to pieces, in order to make the body more manageable for the vultures. Maybe I should have been buried at sea after all and end up with an octopus living in my skull. Now it was too late. It was all too late.

As the prospect of dying became more real, I became more used to the idea, hell I even began to see the good that might come of it. Since the nineties, I had felt that it was my obligation to try and keep the flame of intelligence alive and I was going to be part of, if not spearheading a new Lost Generation.

Back in the 1920's the more creative souls among genteel society had decided to flee the constraints of a depressed postwar America. Prohibition had taken a Svengali-like grip on the nation, and the country was about to be plunged into economical and puritanical darkness as artists, musicians, dancers, sculptors and writers made a run for it. They settled on Paris and at once this proved to be an excellent choice, with Hemmingway, Fitzgerald, Picasso, Joyce and others forming a core of hard-drinking expats who gathered at the home of writer and the self-styled first fan of Cubism, the massively influential Gertrude Stein. Throw Proust, Ravel, Renoir, Monet and Coco Chanel into this creative salad and you can almost taste the atmosphere around the cafes and bars of St Michel and St Germain de Pres. Sadly the magic of Paris of that time had gone and would never come again.

Here I was a hundred years on, in which time it has felt that although humanity has progressed in terms of technology, it has certainly degraded in terms of the intelligence of us as a species, to the point where there was now an active dumbing down of the masses, in the hope of killing off all those who are surplus to the government's needs. First to go would be the unemployable, the career criminal, the disabled, the poor and the mentally ill and to run parallel to this would be a campaign to discredit, dispossess and disenfranchise all those that seek the truth, those who read, those who know better.

I was more aware than most of the advanced state of disrepair our fractured society was in and I wanted no part of it. I would be one of those who needed to be spoken to, to be threatened, to be audited, to be cast out from society with my life's work in tatters if I didn't stay quiet. Worse still, I could die mysteriously in a casual after-dinner walk on a Greek island, or more suspiciously I could end up on the back of a hotel door with my neck wrapped in rope. I will let the reader know in advance that should I ever be found in such a situation, then please understand that it would be not of my own doing. Yes it's true that one time I did fake my own death, though in my defense I was in a fragile place and couldn't see a way out of the doldrums my life had drifted into and though the national press had a field day with the story of my demise, the public on the whole didn't believe a word of it and the scoop had faded by teatime. By the next morning, the whole of the tabloid world had launched their own versions of the game "Where's Sherlock?" with cash incentives being paid for sightings of me and prizes for my capture. The country had split into two factions; first there was the majority of people who had heard the story of my death too many times to now believe that there was even one word of truth in it and the rest could probably be convinced that I had passed away, but certainly not by my own hand. This faction I considered to be my fans, who for whatever reason refused to believe that I would take my own life. Most of them put it down to the size of my ego and if forced to admit it, I would say that they were right in this assumption, though not through me thinking I was too important to die, and the universe couldn't function without me and the whole framework of human existence would come crashing down in the event of my death.

Two hundred years ago, if somebody attempted to take their own life and failed, they were punished heavily for it, as it was deemed as the most selfish of human acts. How could you leave your wife and six children at the gates of the workhouse, the poor house, or on the filthy streets. You madam, how could you possibly leave your husband to look after your six children by himself? How is he going to do that from a debtor's prison? And who's going to cook his tea? The act of self-killing was considered the height of cowardice and self-obsession and was not looked on too kindly at all by either society or the powers that be.

A more contemporary version of this would be to advise the potential suicidee, that though they imagined they were divesting themselves of suffering once and for all, that they were not really getting rid of their pain, but were just passing it on to someone else, namely the loved ones they had left behind. Now if I wasn't a world-renowned detective, with a billionaire industrialist father and a brother who was the Prime Minister's pet and owned a swank private member's club, then I'm quite sure that my death would pass unreported, unlamented and probably if I'm honest, unnoticed. So no, I would never consider taking my own life and yes, the reason would have everything to do with my ego. I wouldn't kill myself for the very simple reason that I would miss me. It was now probably too late for anything to matter. As things stood, I would not be the architect of my own demise and neither would the secret services, who would have soon been breathing down my neck as I slowly outed their secrets. No, not me. My life was to be ended by my best friend, nay my only friend, at my request, not when the government wanted me gone.

If in the future there were any books left to speak of, let alone to read, they would most certainly be heading for the furnace, a tried and tested way of suppressing information. The Chinese, the Romans, the Nazi's, the Catholic church and Henry the Eighth amongst others, had all extinguished their intellectual opposition on the pyre and where the books weren't burned the thinkers were. Now that books were becoming a thing of that past, no doubt the thinkers would again be next in line and while it wouldn't exactly be a blaze to behold, I needed to form a group or at least be a part of one that would a century further on, need to make another run for it. I could leave society to it. I meet brilliant, wonderful, intelligent people all the time as individuals, but as a whole, as a group, as a race, I couldn't stand them and couldn't wait to be rid of them. They could keep their Primark and their pasties and their Hollyoaks and their transgender kids and their modified crops and processed food. They can have it and they can all die in stupid ignorance of the fact that they are being slowly killed off. Why should I care about seven deaths? And why should I save them? Why should I? Save them. Save them. Save them?

Things began to swirl around me. I felt queasy for a second, as my feet were swept away beneath me. At once I was catapulted forward and up and the light became the sun and after that the whole parade of planets, stretching away before me. From circular solids to circular shells and skins, held apart and held together in a gossamer frame. I saw the megalithic sites again, ablaze with light and working how they originally were designed, as power plants. My mind knelt before the equations it faced. Faces came in at the edges to greet me.

First came Ningishzida, Thoth, Hermes, Mercury, with the serpent twisted around his staff. He brought seeds and the plough and all vegetation and I saw he was benevolent and known locally as the Lord of the Good Tree. I knew that he would be a part of my life from now on and whichever path it took. His gentle face faded and was replaced with the blood-shot eyes of Nanna, Osiris, Dionysus, Bacchus and later known simply as Sin.

I saw the excesses of my life, saw the wasted days and nights, the glut, the drugs, the promiscuity and the Caligula-esque rituals I had performed for no more than my own personal enjoyment. I saw the moon he kept and knew that it harnessed the power of the sun for the next civilization to inhabit the earth.

Snapping and snarling, Nergal came next, as Anubis, Hades, Enoch and Metatron and though I quietly thanked him for being the catalyst for me gaining traction with the puzzle, I felt only hatred. I could see the war in him, the death and all the disease he carried. I was further reminded of the evil in me, the fights I had caused and the people I had intentionally hurt. I recognized my aggression and my prior delectation for violence and hoped that this was confined to the past. Before his face faded, I saw him smile.

Marduk, Ra, Horus, Apollo came next, finally a friendly face with something nice to say about me. He was the deity of compassion and justice, and I felt revitalized, happy and hopeful when he looked at me. A wind picked up out of nowhere, turned into a violent mini-cyclone and through it came the face of somebody, who though I was getting to know, looked very much different to the one I knew. It was of course Enlil, Amun, Zeus, Jupiter, Jehovah and though I got no feeling good or bad from him as he passed, no idea what he was the God of, he looked deep into my soul, and I knew it was he who's word cannot be challenged. Thankfully his brother followed.

I was ecstatic to see Enki, Quetzalcoatl, Poseidon,

Neptune and the serpent in the garden. I knew there was no Egyptian equivalent, as he was in South America at the time, setting up his gold mines. He brought wisdom and fresh water. He brought intelligence, healing, art, creation and magic with him. He also brought mischief and I almost wanted to give him a high five when he looked at me. My life should have revolved around this guy, he was everything good and exciting in me and I almost cried tears of joy when, on the way past, he winked at me and laughed.

Last to show was their father Anu, King of all Gods. I saw that he was the dark sun, the sun that rises when this one goes down, the original sun that has no surface to speak of and a core of amber and honey plasma. He told me he was Saturn, lord of the rings and the lord of all creation.

I saw the virtues in man; I saw the gifts that were bestowed on him and how he had squandered it all. I saw this all in a second, less than a second, before I felt myself being dragged the opposite way by my feet. From harp and piano came drums and horns, a cacophony, a torrent of confused noise and discord. I heard howls and cries, cries that became screams and I was hurtling downwards. I finally saw rays of light above or from below, I knew not which, nor now did I care, as I was clearly becoming the change I sought. The screams came to a screeching halt, alongside a sharp pain in my head and the feeling I was choking. I struggled in a blind panic and opened my eyes to see Dr. Watson crouched in front of me and quite visibly upset. He was clasping both of my hands tightly, though he promptly released them to try and foolishly clear my unblocked airway. I was only choking for lack of breath. I greedily gulped down undeserved mouthfuls of air and looked Dr. Watson dead in the eye.

"I know what's missing," I said.

The good doctor was as upset as a person could be, though he made a show of appearing dignified and composed.

"Holmes, don't try to talk. You just rest."

"Watson...Oh my God...that's the most I've ever died," I said, "take me to Angel."

He calmly wiped a single tear away with his jacket sleeve and fell back on his haunches.

"I thought that's where you'd already gone," he said. "How do you feel?"

I beamed at him. "Watson," I said, "nothing can make you feel more alive, than having just died."

Now future retellings of this particular passage of events will put Dr. Watson squarely in the middle as the hero of it all and though there is no doubt that the huge shot of adrenalin he had given me within seconds of delivering yet another potentially fatal payload into my system, had yanked me from the brink, I rather thought my aggressive spirit was the real life-saver here. It was certainly true that the horrific thought of spending eternity with my family had been the catalyst for my sudden revival and without doubt the words "seven lives" had immediately set the alarm bells ringing and reminded me of the task in hand, but if there was one overriding factor and one real hero, then it came from a higher place, as I thought it would have been highly unfair that I should be swept away so cruelly, by a lifestyle I had in all honesty given up. Time had demanded his due and then given me a reprieve. It wasn't time for me to pay my tab...not just yet.

Dr. Watson called Grace, who under my instruction collected and drove a family carrier belonging to a friend in Whitechapel out to where we were in the middle of Buckinghamshire somewhere. I watched from the chair as Dr. Watson and Grace tried to remove the passenger seat. In the end we slid it right back and then lifted me into the space it left, jammed up against the windscreen. Grace drove and Dr. Watson gave a running commentary from the back seat, though he was less scathing in front of Grace. I sat deep in thought and stared at the road that stretched away in the blackness before us.

"Gave me a bloody fright there, Holmes," he mumbled from the back. "I had virtually given you up."

"Excellent, Watson...that's number six."

"What's number six?"

"The seven virtues of man. I was confused by the judge, but all of the victims were paired with a virtue. The banker was prudence, the priest was faith, the judge temperance, the business leader, charity, the politician was fortitude and the singer was hope."

"That's only six."

We turned into a dark, industrial estate. "I know," I said, "here we are."

As we pulled into a small car park, a metal shutter on one of the units rolled up and a large, oily bearded man stood grinning in the doorway. He strode across and yanked my door open. Dr. Watson and Grace exited the van and came to help me get out. I was overjoyed to see him.

"Vincenzo," I said, "is it finished?"

The mechanic just smiled and without a word, reached in and lifted me and the chair out of the van and carried us through into the workshop. He laid the chair carefully on the floor and switched the overhead lights on.

What stood before us was something wonderful. On a small stage area stood a wooden plinth and atop this was a spherical frame made of copper, about two meters tall. On closer inspection one could see that the sphere was split into sections much like an orange and each segment was inscribed beautifully with the lists that I had provided for him. In the center stood three green crystals maybe two feet high, with a space left in between. The whole thing looked mechanical, though I could not distinguish any motors, wires or any potential moving parts.

Vincenzo went to the front of the orb and with a click, opened a door in the front of it. He then came over to me, picked me up again and placed me inside the globe between the crystals. Dr. Watson and Grace looked on without a word, but both rapt at the sidelines. Grace suddenly found her voice.

"So that's what all the texting was about, Sherlock," she said. "You were sending the clues and the dimensions to recreate the puzzle after you smashed the headset." I smiled at her and then at Dr. Watson and finally at Vinny, who was standing by a switch he was ready to throw. He smiled back at me. This was huge for him; he had accepted the mission without hesitation and needed this to work as much as I did for his portfolio.

"You ready?" he said.

I beamed back at him through gritted teeth and nodded. He threw the switch. The orb started to hum and so did I. The copper bands of the machine started to turn independently and slid smoothly and easily within each other, at different depths and at different speeds. I looked around it in wonder, as it seemed to pick up energy. Without starting off the sequence to switch on my receiver, my body began to tingle. I looked down at my arms, still glued to the chair and saw fingers of blue electricity streaming up them. I watched it branch out across my shoulders and envelope my chest. I guess the same had happened with my legs, as the crackling blue veins came up over my knees and streamed into my stomach. The familiar surge of Quidditas rocketed through me, up my chest and my throat and into my head and there was a quiet explosion of light inside me. The copper framework of the sphere slowed and stopped, then a certain part of it started to turn by itself and made a deep grinding noise. One of the copper bands sailed past me and as I watched it, it too stopped and I read the words that were transcribed on it.

Each word was accompanied by a click, as the band settled

into place in the puzzle. PRUDENCE click, FORTITUDE click, FAITH click, TEMPERANCE click, CHARITY click, HOPE click. I smiled as the final virtue sailed into view.... JUSTICE click.

I looked down at my body and I was glowing. Green sparks flew from the crystals that fizzed into me. Blue balls of Torus energy formed in my stomach and my chest, I guessed my throat and head as well, though I couldn't see them. I felt a rare happiness, that was hitherto unknown to me. I looked at Grace and Dr Watson and Vinny, who were watching on in silent awe, and I beamed hopelessly back at them. Tears started to stream down my face.

"I'm in!" I announced, "I'm back in. What do we need. The seven holes in the human head? Seven argonauts? Seven sages of Greece? Seven gates of hell? Seven fountains of nerve energy in the human heart? Or would you like to know that every cell in the human body generates 0.07 milliwatts of electrical energy? Lady and gentlemen, I give you the Seven Rays of Divine Manifestation. The face we present to others and behind it, who we really are...the House that holds the Sun.

The blue lights in my body converged and formed a ball of blue energy in my stomach.

"First ray, PURPOSE, POWER AND WILL" ...click, Second Ray, CONCRETE KNOWLEDGE

AND SCIENCE... click, Third Ray, DEVOTION AND IDEALISM...click, Fourth Ray, HARMONY THROUGH CONFLICT...click, Fifth Ray, ACTIVE INTELLIGENCE...click, Sixth Ray, LOVE AND WISDOM...click and Seventh Ray" .... click.

As we watched, the copper bands began to fade and were replaced with images of the words they represented. Faces of Sumerian Gods started to spin around me. Nergal looked livid, Anu divine. Planets began to spin on their axes and then around the sphere, all kinds of geometric shapes started to spin around, as did megalithic sites, beautiful sounds and colors began to merge in harmonic resonance, shafts of light reached out and connected everything and this whole mini world was bathed in golden light.

I looked up and I saw the puzzle in its entirety minus the star coming down from the sky. Slowly I started to stand. My body came away slowly but easily from the chair, until I stood up tall, raised my face to the skies and opened my mouth, exposing my throat. The blue sphere above my head started to collapse and then poured itself down my throat and joined up all the lights still fizzing through my body. The light then formed a blue ball again, shot back out of my throat and floated just above my head, where it spun, feeding itself from the inside. I closed my throat and stood imperious, grinning down at my friends, who were still in utter shock at what was unfolding before them. Before I could take a single step, I looked down at my feet, just in time to see them begin to disappear. "Whoa!" I shouted, "look at me! I'm off! I'll see you later, Watson."

Dr. Watson looked on in bewilderment. Grace stood gaping.

"It's real," she whispered, "it's all real."

"Holmes, where the devil are you going?"

I was ecstatic. "I have no idea, Watson. Wherever Dorian is. I'll bring Chinese back.... Singapore noodles was it? Only gather what you can carry, Watson. You get to take it with you! And remember, *nothing* is what it is, Watson, and there are two of everything!" I felt a strong urge to sing and as the cells in my body began to transmutate, my body began to disappear, and I started to sing at the top of my voice.

"Give me oil in my lamp, keep me burning, give me oil in my lamp I pray."

Grace, Dr. Watson and Vinny stood and stared at a large empty space. The sphere had gone, the blue ball had gone and according to later reports, in a brilliant flash of light, so had I.

CHAPTER FIFTEEN

BRITANNIA WAIVES THE RULES

When I resurfaced, I was standing towards the rear of a small, thick clump of trees. All around this copse, the land spread far away and was flat and featureless, apart from one structure I knew all too well, which in turn cast a forbidding shadow towards me. The rains had stopped and now kicked up the most vivid and pleasant odors, which as individual smells brought with them their own memories on the air. Much the same as a prize bull or a big cat would do, I leaned my head back and thrust my nose into the air, taking in each individual smell up my nose, while at the same time curling my lip and reading every scent that came in on the breeze.

Each of the smells were accompanied briefly with their own particular story, though nothing in detail, just a snapshot of a brief history of the smell and a synopsis of what that fragrance meant to me. Wet woodland aromas of moss and bark came in as a thick band and was all-pervading, was everywhere, under and around and all other smells came in on brief narrow spikes. Blowing in from out of the copse, was the smell of stone and moorland and rain of different varieties, stair-rods that came straight down and battered the turf into mud and some lighter angled drizzle that had always just stopped and was always just about to start.

There was something else I took in up through my synapses and into my head was the smell of panic, of fright, of fear and the smell of sadness. Not an established smell of sadness, though much like the woodland, the all-encompassing scent, under and around was an ancient sadness, a historical melancholy that would never be gone. The brief narrow spikes that came through that were of fear of now, fear of immediate danger, a fear and fright so fresh and only felt in the innocent and in the young.

As I watched, twenty or so hooded figures traipsed slowly in single file, heads bowed towards the stone structure. Just by the statures of the figures, I could tell they were a mixture of male and female. A few carried burning torches, though in the moonlight they proved to be entirely ceremonial. They did march slowly in a single line, apart from four men in the middle who carried a sedan laced with golden filigree. On the chair of the sedan sat a young girl of maybe nine years old, immoveable, frozen and dressed in white. She was blindfolded and gagged and had her hands tied in front of her. The group headed slowly into the center of the stone structure and almost out of sight.

I had to get closer without breaking the cover of the trees and to do that I needed to make my way to the edge of the copse over to the left. As I lifted my foot to take a step, something glinted in my eye in the exact spot I intended to go and as my eyes adjusted, I made out a figure dressed in black, lying full-length at the edge of the wood.

The person had removed something long and metallic from a dark bag and had settled down back in the grass, focused on the group. A large, sleek black car pulled slowly into view and parked by the side of the copse. Two men in black emerged from the front of the car, one of them scoured the area and the other opened the rear car door. A figure stepped from the car and was passed a cowled cloak, which they draped over themselves and all three followed the group towards the stone structure.

Before the automatic lights of the car dimmed, I glanced back at the figure lying in the grass and expected to hear a shot and watch the middle of the three fall but none of this occurred and I soon found out why. The dimming lights of the car had lit up that part of the forest and before they switched off entirely, I recognized who the sniper was. It was the mortuary assistant and though he was indeed about to take somebody out, it wasn't the person who had just arrived, but I knew that they would be the next and the last. I stared towards the group, straining my eyes to see. She was in there somewhere. I knew what was coming next and I wanted Grace and Dr. Watson to watch too. Maybe they needed help getting there. I stood calmly behind a tree and started to turn my receiver on.

I resurfaced on the back seat of the family carrier. Grace was driving and Dr. Watson and I were playing with an I-pad and now and again checking the road in front of them. They were trying to figure out the rest of the puzzle by themselves, bless them. Mindful of the fact that I needed to be gentle so as not to arouse suspicion from Dr. Watson, I opened my eyes, reappeared in the copse and instantly reset myself for a gentle trip into the good doctor's mind once more. When I came back, I was sitting next to Grace, staring through the windscreen, as the provincial suburbs started to become countryside again. I looked down at the screen. Dr. Watson had taken a photograph of the wall in the shithole and was strangely quiet. Perfect. I crept in.

"There is two of everything...and nothing is what it is," he said, "nothing is what it is. It's in the letters again. It's the bloody letters."

I faced the front and kept relatively quiet; I didn't want Watson to know I was there. I smiled to myself, as he continued.

"It wasn't EMP. Well, it was both. Look how they are written on the wall, they are in the form of a triangle... member of the European parliament. The first one, the one who got away...Price...Ellie-Mae Price."

Grace stared at the darkness in front of her. "Okaaay, what's the next one."

Dr Watson grunted. "Ah, maybe I'm mistaken, the next one was the number of a flight." "Where to?"

"Alaska. Where Sherlock has sent Mycroft."

"Oh, when I saw that, I thought it meant frequency 432HZ, the frequency of the human body. But that makes sense. And MF? If that's not magnetic force, or magnetic field, then what is it? And what is MOD if it isn't Ministry of Defense?

"MOD, if I know Sherlock, means Master of Disguise. MF stands for Male and Female, but not Sherlock. HA and RP are together but aren't anywhere in Alaska. I personally thought it referred to a musical harp, but I think it's something else."

Grace started to get excited. "It's also a star system," she said, "look that up."

Watson was already on it. I let him go, as it would have been too obvious for me to solve the whole thing for him. He made his little search on the i-pad, then stopped suddenly and stared at Grace. She smiled back at him.

"The harp star," he said and held up the screen. He stared straight ahead. "Lyra." I beat a hasty retreat, back to the copse, but this time I imagined that I was at the edge of the trees. It was a strange sensation when I appeared there, as I could also see myself standing further back in the middle of the wood, fizzing blue.

I watched the sniper remove the hood and then also remove her blue wig. From that standpoint and though I was out of human earshot, I could see everything and could hear every word.

The young girl had been led to a stone table, which two of the cloaked figures lifted her on to. Her hands were untied from in front of her and were held with straps attached to both sides of it. My heart ached for her. A large figure moved towards the center of the group and stood now at the head of the table. They were offered a curved dagger on a cushion from one of the minions, which they took and raised to the sky.

"We mortify the flesh, to purify the soul," they said.

As the figure lifted the dagger, their face got caught in the moonlight. Though the size of the figure suggested it was a man, I knew before I saw her, that I was watching the High Priestess, our elusive politician, the formidable Elli-Mae Price. She continued.

"And by living in the darkness, we move ever closer to your light."

She raised the dagger high over the child and paused. The dagger slipped from her hands, and she stood stock still, her cruel eyes wide and staring. A thin trickle of blood started to run from the hole that had just appeared in the middle of her forehead, and she pitched forward and fell dead on her face.

At once, the two men who skulked on the edges of the structure raced forward and made a dive for their ward and together they smothered him and ghosted him away and back to the car. The rest of the group scattered in all directions, some taking cover behind the standing stones, but most made a beeline for the copse I now emerged from.

As some sped past me in panic, the cowls that hid their faces blew back and I made a mental note of each of their faces. I adjusted the hood on my cloak and walked purposefully towards the structure. I made straight for the stone table on which the little girl was strapped and started to untie her hands. Once freed, she fell into my arms, and I scooped her up and held her with all my strength.

One other figure remained and I approached them, and we both looked down at the politician lying prostrate on the ground, her black eyes still registered the shock they had when she was shot. The wind had picked up. I removed my hood and the blue wig, then put the child down, took off the cloak and wrapped her in it, then picked her up again and held her close.

"You let him go?" I asked, as I watched the dignitary being bundled into the car and whisked away from the scene before the police arrived. Dorian removed the hood from his cloak and stared after the speeding car. He smiled.

"We'll catch up with him tomorrow. Hello, Sherlock."

He turned to face me, and we stared at each other for some time. From the far side of the copse, I saw several vehicles racing away from the scene and at the same time heard the wail of sirens of the police who were inevitably racing this way. With only one road in and out, I figured that everybody would be stopped, apart from the man who left first. He would not be detained.

I wondered why he said that "we" would catch up with him. If he split into two again and Bad Dorian found him first, then I would still fail the mission, and everyone would still die. The genial chap that stood before me who was good and bad, but at the same time a human being in his own right named Dorian was the person I wanted to know. I felt that with the saving of Lucy, that Dorian and I had broken new ground, after he watched the harrowing report of Theresa. We had found a common link of empathy, but I knew I would be a fool to let my guard down. I wanted to know this person and to trust them, but I knew that I couldn't. I also couldn't think too much, as he knew every word that passed through my mind. All too late, as those thoughts themselves had already been heard and processed by him.

"You could have easily killed him here," I said. "Why did you let him go?"

He smiled at me. "Who knows, Sherlock. Maybe I wanted you to find me first. I knew you were close. How do you know it's a he?"

"I just had to find out what was missing," I replied.

"And now you have a new box of tricks. Magic is waiting for you, Sherlock. You have emerged victorious, but only if the work is carried on. You know that you have a duty to do what's right. I trust I am leaving my work in capable hands?"

I smiled at him like a fool, "You are."

"I'll be watching, Sherlock," he said.

I watched the red filaments spread across his eyeballs and his nose sharpened and become more pronounced. The generous, ready smile dropped in to a haggard sneer and the voice lost its lilt and gathered menace. Enlil's malevolent image pushed itself out of Enki's and stared horribly at me, looking from one eye to the other.

"And so will I," he growled.

As he uttered these words, Stonehenge sprang to life all around us. The ancient monument began to emit a low vibration in its usual key of F, corresponding to and in harmony with the heart chakra. To a trained ear, the note began to change and settled on F#Major, the sharp note on the way to G that corresponded with the throat Chakra and denoted a change in mankind, a transition stage in the evolution of our species, one that was harmonized beautifully and exhibited in many megalithic sites around the world, including the Great Pyramid. The progression from F# to G was happening to the Earth, but as I listened, I knew that every man and woman would be responsible for their own transition, the building of their own spiritual ark and in charge of their own procession to the next dimension. The Slaughter Stone and the rest of the Sarsens took on an amber glow, that on a cloudy, rain-filled day obviously wasn't due to the sun. The lintels lit up next and all across the top of the Sarsens, they shimmered in a honey-colored haze.

Blue forks of electricity begin to stream through Dorian's body and they grew in intensity. The good and the bad merging together and growing together out of the flesh, the silver and blue melting into the orange and black. They rose together, morphed into one, ten feet high and turned gold. I put Lucy gently on the ground and held her hand, as we both looked up at Dorian. Dr Watson and Grace emerged from the tree line and strode towards us. I handed Lucy to Grace and as one, we all turned our faces to Dorian. Thick rays of light poured down from the sky and joined with the band of gold that had wrapped the monument in pure harmonic resonance and with a quick glance and a smile at me, there was a bright flash of light and Enki and Enlil, the messiah and the monster were gone, leaving Dorian the man standing small and unsure and looking about him in perfect wonder and bewilderment.

"Where the fuck am I?" he demanded in a heavy East London accent. He directed his unlettered tirade specifically at me and closed the gap between us. "Do you know who I fucking am?" he growled.

The face that I had grown to respect and love had sadly gone; that genial spark in the eyes had been replaced with a milky, opaque film that told me this man was ill. The smooth tanned skin was mottled with busted blood vessels and pitted with old scars and unhealed scabs, and the serene demeanor of my former host now reverted to its original state of breathless anger and unreasonable impatience, caused by heart disease and liver damage. I missed Enki like I once missed Irene and as I stared into the dying eyes of this jumped-up little gangster, I started to wonder about a voluntary death at the hands of Enlil and how favorable it would be, as opposed to extending the existence of this miserable creature and his kind on this beautiful planet.

Dr. Watson approached me and forgetting himself, almost addressed me cheerfully, but we knew something was broken and he remembered his anger in time. He looked sheepish, but afforded me a quick, thin smile.

"You did it, Holmes," he announced.

"I haven't really done anything, Watson. If anyone has done anything, then it's you. Only remarkable detective work has brought you here."

Dr. Watson. snorted. "I thought that at first," he said. "But apart from following the grape juice, Sherlock, how much of it did I actually solve by myself?"

I ignored him and started to walk towards the people carrier. Police cars and vans were pulling up all around us now...it was time for me to go.

"More than you know, John," I said as I walked off, "more than you know."

If a person's knowledge is the sum total of everything they have ever experienced, then that alone would be the reason I have been historically regarded as one of the country's leading minds and not for my powers of deduction, I suggest. Universally renown for my debonair style and love of unusual clothes, wine, music, artwork and places, I have never sought to surround myself with the trappings of a privileged lifestyle. I don't collect things, I don't store, I don't save and I don't stock. Things are not my thing, I am a collector of experiences, through which I gain dimension and through dimension, character and therein lies the key to my success as an accurate observer of the human condition. I looked at every day as a brand-new adventure, for I truly believed that life should be treated in as much the same way as a working holiday, being present in every moment, never regretting the past, nor being overly troubled by what lies ahead.

As I have stated before, I have needed to confront the darkness in myself in order to see and understand the darkness in others. How else could I equalize the current winter within me? How could I coax the massed ranks from the shadows to address their collective shame, if I couldn't still the demons that lurked in my individual soul. Hopefully the balance had been redressed, and I could finally find some peace from the Jungian stew that sloshed around inside my head. Or if it's a stew, would that be Jungarian? I didn't know any more...and I didn't care. I let myself into 221b Baker Street and climbed the stairs with all the enthusiasm of a man going to the gallows.

CHAPTER SIXTEEN

REFUGIA

Mrs. Hudson was sitting in my living room by the window, playing sudoku. She would often spend a few hours there if I was away for any length of time, as my flat got the low afternoon sun and as she said that she suffered from some kind of light-deprivation disorder. Whether I believed in such an ailment or not, I respected her decision to do something about it. She would wake with the sun in her own apartment and sit for an hour under a series of lights if there was no sun to speak of and if she was feeling melancholy in the afternoon, then it was another bout under the lights or a siesta in my window. I did believe her, as it happens, though I didn't believe for a second that sudoku was a game. A game of mathematics? I knew she hated math for the same reason most people do and that was because she didn't understand it but used it to try to keep her mind sharp. Nowadays it could be posited that people hate math because, as the Italians say, that "math isn't an opinion" and more than anything people today need to have an opinion, without really having anything to say.

She turned to greet me, as I removed my hat and coat with

a sigh and walked over to my armchair. It felt so good to sit down in my own home. She obviously wasn't her normal

chatty self and neither was I, so for a few minutes I stared at the clock on the mantlepiece, while Mrs. Hudson stared at the sun. She turned her face towards me and smiled. She looked weary.

"Are you okay, Sherlock? Are you hungry?"

I smiled and shook my head. I was starving but I didn't need to disrupt her afternoon. She looked shattered, but I didn't say anything...you don't do you. Normally I would have done. There were many better ways to phrase it without being rude or offending her.

"It rained a lot last night," I said. "Did you sleep okay?"

Mrs. Hudson continued with her puzzle. "Not really, Sherlock...I think there are penguins in the attic."

She hadn't changed. I gave it a few seconds and then said. "Surely you mean pigeons, Mrs. Hudson."

She looked surprised. "Why, what did I say?"

"You said penguins!"

She didn't bat an eyelid. She looked out onto the street. "You never know, Sherlock...it could be penguins. What about that one in Wallace and Gromit? He was a nasty piece of work. Jewel thief I think he was. You never know, there could be a whole load of them up there waiting for us to fall asleep so they can burgle us. Magpies...they're thieves too. I wonder what it is about black and white birds. Well, they can help themselves, they won't get anything from me, I've got no jewelry left to steal...you've eaten it all."

I smiled to myself and closed my eyes. I loved Mrs. Hudson and I was happy she was here. My body finally started to drop, as it began to let go of the stress that had paralyzed me for the past week.

"Oh, I forgot to say congratulations, Sherlock." The sunshine had given her a boost, though I knew she hadn't had enough of the therapy and was just pretending for me, as she now felt like she invading my space. I opened my eyes as she got up from the window.

"What for?"

"Dr. Watson said that you were getting back into your mind palace. I wanted to send you a message, but you're here now." She walked over to me and gave me a quick peck on the cheek.

"I just wanted to say Bon Voyage, Sherlock. I'll go and make you some food."

And with this she left the room.

I thought how hard that must have been for her. I hadn't been losing my memory, though had temporarily lost all access to it and at the same time Mrs. Hudson was slowly ravaged by the dementia that was destroying her faculties and eating her alive. All being well, it would only be a brief hiccup for me, but for her it was a one-way ticket, there would be no return journey for her, and here she was wishing me a safe trip back and making me a meal. At times it had been funny to see and hear us, as we both went beautifully bonkers, but now it hit me hard and in my own living room chair I broke. I broke for the things I had been through in this case, and I broke at the thought of what I had to do, I broke for our species and the future it didn't deserve. I broke easily and simply and just in two pieces, but I shattered like a diamond in a meteor strike when I thought about Mrs. Hudson and the size of her heart and I curled up right there in the chair and cried my fucking eyes out.

The next morning, I woke up crumpled on my chair with the sun streaming through the window and half of my face burned off. As usual I played my little game of guessing the time before looking at the clock on the mantlepiece, though I guessed the time and just didn't bother looking for two reasons. Firstly, because I knew that time mattered less to me than it ever did and secondly, because I knew I was right. Exactly right. Mrs. Hudson hadn't yet made an appearance, though she had obviously been back the night before with my food, as it lay congealed on the table beside me. I gathered that emotion had overtaken her too and she had probably crept silently to her rooms and sobbed herself to sleep, just as I had done. If she was sleeping in, then good, I would leave her and go about mine and everybody else's business.

I slipped on my suede loafers, had my breakfast shot, brushed my teeth and stole quietly down the stairs and out on to Baker Street.

Though still early, it was muggy and moist and uncomfortable, it was like walking into a cake. I grabbed a cheap pair of sunglasses from one of those places that only sells quaint English relics and jostled my way to the tube station. I sent a text to Grace and shuffled my way with the throb of oily shoppers down the dirty ancient steps of the Bakerloo line and waited among the rank and vile for the tube to Charing Cross, on which when it arrived, I found myself a corner of and took in the huddled masses. With the benefit of sunglasses, I was able to observe closely the subjects I was meant to save from extinction, without anybody noticing, though being in a train under the ground and wearing shades, I was probably attracting more attention than I normally would. The Roman poet, Juvenal in his work Satire X, had suggested that in order to curtail the public's desires, they needed only two things and they would never revolt, these being bread and circuses and as I looked around the cramped carriage, I found it ironic that apart from the passengers who were blatantly from somewhere else and talked excitedly to each other, the rest wore faces devoid of expression and all had, as the Spanish say, "un cara de pan"...a bread face. A few minutes later we screeched to a stop at Charing Cross and every single person made for the exit.

I truly did believe that Irene and I were meant for each other. We had all the attributes of a couple destined for happiness together, but my ability to nurture and protect what we had, was non-existent and died over time, like the flower you forgot to water. The things I loved about her, I continued to love, though it was only after she died that I realized that I only loved in her the exact same things that I loved in myself. I never looked for her to complete me, to be full of characteristics I lacked, to round off my edges and introduce me to new experiences. No, I recognized myself in her and that was it. She thought Mozart was autistic, Schumann was bi-polar and Wagner had a problem with jews, which I thought was interesting and quite probably true. Her taste in clothes was refined and elegant and strictly displayed no brand logos, no motifs, no labels, all of which were cut out, as were mine. Her love of art, on a much smaller scale, progressed precisely as it had for the rest of the planet, though I know now that her work of any given period wasn't a folly or a fad, but was a direct reflection of how she felt about her life at the time.

When I first met her, I looked at her work the same way I looked at her furniture. Her apartment was crammed with Renaissance, Baroque and Rococo furniture and her paintings were depressing, with dark colors, shadow play and heavy brush strokes. I thought she just loved Caravaggio, as did I... and she did, but the sadness and the violence depicted in her work, was her exorcising the demon that was her father and not her love for the period. After a few Gaudi-inspired months dabbling in the Art Nouveau movement, we hit a purple patch in our relationship, and she escaped from her studio as much as she could.

We took regular trips to the countryside in the fairer months and to the South of France in the colder ones, so that she could paint outside. We were at our happiest, driving the twisting roads of the Cote D'Azur, looking past the Jasmine fields for rivers that ran to the sea, which we would then follow back up until we found a stream, and we would lay our blanket on the grass and eat cheese and drink wine, and I would watch her paint and smell the flowers till the sun went down.

This was to be her Romantic period and the time I remember when I was also at my happiest. From there, there was a quick jump through Cubism before it got too silly, straight into Surrealism and Abstract Expressionism, where she retired to her studio once more, emptied the apartment of all furniture and started flinging paint all over the walls. I failed supremely to notice her frustration in me and that my chaotic life was the cause of her anger and resentment and her cry for help, and when she went back and finally settled on the watery colors and short, impatient brush strokes of the impressionists, with the work all having a feeling of being unfinished and uncared for, I didn't realize, didn't notice and didn't feel that that was when she had given up on us.

It lasted longer than it should have, but only down to a lack of awareness on my part. We found it hard to let each other go and I ended up playing hard to get rid of, so life intervened disguised as death. It wasn't meant to last no matter how suited we were; my relationships are volatile and burn themselves out quickly, as do my friendships, because I believed that the longer you are involved in a person's life and the more you rely on each other, the greater the pain you inflict when you leave, and I would much rather make a mark than leave a hole. What I realized much later was that the mark sometimes became a stain; now every hole can be filled, but some stains can never be removed, which is why after the death of Irene, I fell into the clutches of the night and into the company of the ladies who dwelt there. They expected nothing except money from me, which is precisely what they got, though when the lockdown hit, I longed for the touch of a woman, not for the sloppy indiscretions I had become accustomed to on the rebound, but the closeness, the touch and smell of the skin and the maddening conversations.

During the pandemic, the numbers of couples splitting up had sky-rocketed, which made me feel severely lonely. It wasn't fair...I didn't have anybody. I wanted someone to split up with. I missed Irene and I missed being in a relationship and as I sat on the rooftop terrace of The View, looking down onto the crowd that had gathered in Trafalgar Square, I saw Grace emerging from the fringes and entering the ground floor of the bar I watched her from. I could go all in with Grace. She was independent, but not a militant feminist, she was beautiful without thinking or knowing it. She was funny without being goofy, full of facts but retained a rabid thirst for knowledge. She was feminine, though was a more than competent joiner, plumber, painter and all-round physical hard worker.

I imagined myself with her and I saw myself happy. What if we ran off together and forgot all about finishing the puzzle? What if I let the day just go on and I allowed the celebrations to unfold in the city without mishap?

What if I turned my back on Enki and Enlil just to see what happened? It wouldn't take long for Enlil to find me, but in that short space of time I would be happy, right up to the point where everybody died. We could hide out in Provence and have our wine and sandwiches by the river. I could recreate the only time in my life where I was truly content. That is until Enlil found me and ended it all, but at least I wouldn't die alone....and of course I could call it my Grace period.

I have always wondered if the joy of love is worth the pain of loss and the answer has always been yes, yes, a thousand times yes. If Grace and I got married and were blissfully happy for six months, I would consider it worth it. She wanted me, but she wanted me to settle down.

Sadly, as with all my relationships, somebody more attentive would come into her life and, while I loved the fact that Grace wanted me to go down on one knee, I knew right in that instant, that again, as with all previous relationships, that I would end up on both.

Seneca and Marcus Aurelius watched and waited and I chuckled to myself. Would instant gratification and short-term personal pleasure be justified if I could hold this feeling forever and recall it at will, when I was down and lonely and desired someone's touch, as I can now with Irene. Probably, but all future memories would soon be outlawed and under control of the government and besides, desire, it is said, will only lead to suffering. Oh pilgrim, I'm afraid it's much simpler than that.

When all is said and done, desire *is* suffering.

On the other hand, I could turn my back on Grace and all future happiness with a partner.

I could finish the puzzle, but then what? I would still be me but would no longer be the Sherlock Holmes the world knew and loved. Without doubt I would still be burdened with the title and the occupation, though the essence of me would be gone. Again, not in the eyes of my adoring public, but to me, as I would no longer have nor need the power of deduction, as I would know everything. Every case would be solved immediately, without it ever being necessary for me to explain how I reached my conclusion. As in mathematics, it's all very well and good having the final answer, but I needed to show my working out and the steps it took for me to get there. I would elevate myself from the rank of consulting detective to wizard and the world would applaud me, and my services would be sought the world over and I would be the first new human off the production line, an androgynous chimera, with nothing to feel and with nobody to love. But I would hate myself. I wouldn't be able to explain how I worked it out, how I saw the minute details that everybody else overlooked. I suppose I could pretend that I was still using the power of deduction, by immediately knowing the answer, keeping it to myself and then reverse-engineering the problem, to show everyone how I had arrived at my conclusion. This case had shown me how that could be achieved, as there had been minimal deduction needed to solve it. I would be too much. And that wouldn't be enough.

As soon as Grace sat down, I knew she wasn't comfortable. She gave me a quick smile and looked around nervously. Even before my newly acquired skill of knowing what people are thinking, I knew what she was thinking, though this time I could actually hear the words as she thought them and I went off her ever so slightly, as I listened to her curse like a sailor for the next minute or so.

"Where have all these people come from?" she pondered, "fucking Royalists." She moved forward in her chair as a couple of large women squeezed by. Grace smiled sweetly at them both.

"You could get a tank through there," she mused.

She smiled at the girls again and then flashed her eyes at me, pulled her chair closer to the table and looked behind herself again. "There you go, chunks, wasn't that hard, was it? I'd better order before you eat everything."

She smiled quizzically at me...." What?" ... "What's happened? What did I do? It's busy in here."

I gazed back at her and smiled and shook my head. I should have stood up and pulled her chair out for her, but there was nowhere to pull it to, and it would have just complicated matters, so I never bothered to offer. Instead, I grabbed the wine menu and pretended to read it.

"It's busy everywhere. The Prince of Bohemia is in town,"

I said without looking at her. I caught one of the beleaguered waiter's eyes and ordered a bottle of Margaux. Grace finally settled in her seat, spread her hands in front of her on the white linen and gave me a weak smile.

"And the Princess," she added. "I thought you had stopped drinking...special occasion?" she asked a little too sarcastically, as she gazed intently at the menu. "What are you having? I'm starving."

I ignored the question and glanced idly around the bedlam in the room. What was set out to be and indeed till now was, a private club for the more discerning members of the movie industry, had been transformed for the day into a cross between a hospital waiting room and a bingo hall, where half the room was in the way of the other half, who were either on one of their frequent trips to the toilet, were still settling in or were waiting for their milky lattes to go cold. I didn't want to be here, but it was vital if I wanted to have a future with Grace, however brief that future turned out to be. I snapped my attention back to the table, steepled my fingers under my chin and beamed at Grace.

"I'm not hungry now," I said. "I was ravenous when I got here, but I have totally lost my appetite." I looked around briefly. "The food isn't leaving the kitchen quickly either, I've been watching. Every other order is a toasted teacake.... they're everywhere. If I was you, I would order something cold, or order somewhere else...unless you want a toasted teacake. It smells of wet dogs and lavender in here."

Grace had a final look at the menu. "And piss and biscuits." I heard her think. Probably overjoyed to have a couple of normal paying customers, he hovered by the table, waiting for Grace to choose. She finally set the menu down and turned to him.

"Thanks, but I'm not that hungry...can I just get a latte and a toasted teacake please." On the surface, it looked like the waiter took the menu from her, bowed ever so slightly and disappeared with her order. What really happened was that as soon as Grace had delivered her choice, I felt the disappointment in the waiter, like a blow to the stomach. I saw how hard he was trying this morning. I saw that he had been called in on his day off and agreed to it because he not only because he was new here, felt he had to and needed the wage, but this month needed every extra penny he could get his hands on for his new house and the baby he was about to become a father to.

Large events in the city always required extra staff and would usually land every staff member more than three times their salary in tips. Alas this wasn't the Spice Girls reforming, this wasn't Dancing on Ice, this wasn't a Movie Premiere, nor the well-heeled customer base that goes with those crowds. This was the loyal legion of fans that followed religion and followed the Royals, wherever they were from. They were to a man, over seventy, drank slowly, ate hardly anything and left no tip whatsoever.

I could feel the anguish in the waiter as he walked away deflated. I felt somewhat to blame, as I suppose my not eating anything and my grim assessment of the service had probably swayed Grace in her decision to behave like a pensioner. Not to worry, as I'm sure that the management had got teacakes in especially for this occasion, as they weren't on the normal menu, but were advertised on a small card on the table, that come midday, would be turned inside out to offer a scone with jam and clotted cream in its place. They had catered for this. Not only had they catered for this, but they were getting their scones bought in at fourteen pence each, twelve pence each for the jam and cream portion and a few pence for indirect overheads like freezer storage, transport and labor, with a gross profit margin set at seventy percent, the price should not have gone north of two pounds fifty. As they were listed at nearly seven pounds, I decided that the management knew exactly what they were doing and if they sold three hundred teacakes and four hundred scones today, then they would make the best part of five grand on those two items alone, which wasn't bad for a Monday and this lot would be tucked up in bed by eight o'clock, at which point they could reset the restaurant and the bar for normal service and make a quick ten grand on cocktails and champagne later tonight. I still felt sorry for the waiter though, as he showed me the label on the bottle and then poured me a taste.

I brought the wine to my nose and breathed it in, lowered the glass and then brought it back again. Complex wines will often give different flavor profiles as they "open up," sometimes changing by the sip and on the rare occasion like now, with every smell and every sniff. I swirled the glass and closed my eyes. Cabernet Sauvignon and ten percent Merlot. As it didn't reveal everything on the first sniff, it couldn't be a new world wine, now showing dark fruit, leather and tobacco and given a bit of backbone by the oak barrels it was aged in before bottling. The sweetness of the cherries and cassia were shot through with perfect acidity, keeping it fresh and sharp before the vanilla came along. It was balanced, aged well, earthy and mature, a perfectly delightful Bordeaux all being said. The giveaway, however, was that the bottle had arrived at the table opened and that, along with the waiter's now obviously disinterested manner and my ability to read his mind, told me that he had taken a mid-priced St Julien Chateau Lagrange and had decanted it into an empty expensive Chateau Margaux bottle and in revenge for him not making any money from our table, had tried to palm off the lesser wine on me.

Wrong house, wrong street, young man. This poor guy's bad day was about to get a whole lot worse. I looked up at him, and he knew that I knew. The smile that was painted uneasily across his face, flattened out under the strain.

"How is it, Sir?" he asked, hopefully.

I continued to look into his eyes, just until I felt that Grace was about to admonish me for being rude.

"It's excellent," I replied, taking another sip, "but it's not a Margaux. Can I see the cork?"

I could have let the whole thing slide, I suppose. Nobody died. The waiter had decided, whether it was the house policy or not, to try to make some money for his little family and I didn't begrudge him that one bit. Quite the opposite, I silently applauded the man for his initiative and had his little scheme paid off, then he would have had a seven-hundred-pound bottle of wine to sell. I quietly brought his little stunt to the attention of his manager, who, knowing very well who I was, almost threw himself at my knees at the thought of getting the local police and newspapers involved.

He told me the waiter's backstory in groveling, heart-breaking detail, how he was new and blamed himself for not dealing with my table personally and promised me membership for life (which I already had, due to my brother's connections with the Diogenes.) He offered me a bottle of Margaux on the house, which I refused as the experience had soured my palate and promised me all number of things to drop the complaint. Yes, I could have let it slide, could have fallen for the ruse and been out of pocket for a great cause. I could afford it. The waiter could have got a crib for the baby and something nice for his girlfriend. They could have had a trip away, or just not worried for a week or two. I could also easily have had a quiet word in the waiter's ear and told him the game was up, to which he would fetch me the correct wine and then wonder what to do with the original. Worst case scenario was he would have to pay for it himself and be thirty-five pounds out of pocket.

Things didn't pan out that way though...in reduced straits, his girlfriend would move back with her parents, and he would develop a heroin habit, from which there would be no way back. His relationship would end when the baby was born and after a few drunken phone calls to the mother, he would not be allowed near her or his child at all. The new furniture would all be sold, the house repossessed and he would die from a massive overdose, without ever holding his son. All that caused by one moment of madness. Just one. And yes, I'll say it again, I could have forgotten all about it and let the scenario unfold in a multitude of ways and none would have ended so badly. It wasn't the money and it wasn't the crime that bothered me. The fact that I was embarrassed in Grace's company only troubled me slightly and only slightly more than the discomfort I felt having everyone in the restaurant furiously trying to tweak their hearing-aids and lean in for the gossip. No, all that I could let slide. What I couldn't forgive the waiter for at all was thinking that I didn't know the difference between a mid-range Bordeaux and a Chateau Margaux.

Grace made a point of paying her bill and together, we launched ourselves into the flag-waving, deckchair-carrying throng that was filling up the way to Trafalgar Square. She put her arm through mine, smiled up at me and clung to me as we made a left, crossed over Cockspur Street and made a right on Pall Mall, back towards the square. The road was closed and lined with people. Slowly, a cortege of Bentleys and Rolls Royces made its way down the street to the delight of the crowd, who had braved the weather to be there.

Grace and I continued to walk behind the crowd, and it felt good to have her hold me, though truth be told she was really just holding on to me. And I knew right there. I knew I could be happy with Grace. She was everything I wasn't and I, likewise, was nothing like her. But we were perfect together, but only for now. I knew it wouldn't take long for Enlil to find me, I couldn't hide from him and I knew it. It could be a year or two before he brought the next flood, or asteroid, or disease or whatever charming method of extinction our pathetic race was earmarked for, before we expanded beyond this realm. Or he could find me immediately and I would probably end up threaded through some medieval torture device... and it would serve me right.

The cortege crawled closer and we both turned slightly to see the Royals waving from their car. Somewhere along the way, they were supposed to stop and greet the crowd, but that was probably further up on the Strand, or in the square itself. Just then the front car stopped, the rear doors opened and they both exited, the Princess of Bohemia, with her dazzling smile on this side and the Prince on the other and they made straight for the crowds.

They both wore all black and wore huge smiles, as they each approached their well-wishers on either side of the street. I had only ever seen the Princess in the press, and it was her that the people had come to see.

They shrieked and curtseyed and gave her flowers and cards, which she passed to her lady-in-waiting, who followed close behind. He, on the other hand I knew very well and though I only seen him once in the dark, with either a blanket thrown over his head, or wearing a hood, I could smell him. I could hear the chatter in his depraved head and the smile he gave to the crowd was more of a showing of teeth, a grimace that turned down at the mouth and never went near the eyes. Just a smile, but for me it was a call to arms. I saw in photonic detail every sordid transgression he had inflicted on the innocent children brought to his palace, the torture, the misery, the destruction of innocence and inside I caught fire.

After reviewing CCTV footage of the crowds on Pall Mall, the police would have no choice but to arrest me for the kidnap and grisly murder of the Prince of Bohemia, and though the evidence would be circumstantial, it would also be very compelling. Slowed down, the footage from the procession on the packed street would indeed show the prince and I disappear from sight at the exact same moment, though the frames couldn't be slowed down enough to render a clear image. One blurred figure kidnaps another blurred figure, so what? I would rightly argue that that could have been anyone and I would be right. Luckily there would also be video evidence of Grace and I at various times and locations throughout London for the rest of the day, including the precise moment that the prince seemingly vanished into thin air, which would baffle Scotland Yard all ends up, and seeing as I had neither a twin, nor the ability to just disappear, plus the fact that I was protected by sovereign and diplomatic immunity, they would be forced, against my brother's wishes to finally let me go.

But right now, as I sauntered through Hyde park with Grace, I saw the future of civilization unfold in my head. I saw the privileged few would in turn poison and starve three quarters of the planet's population. I saw their murderous agenda pressed into the hands and mouths of a dumbed-down society, who had no understanding of what they were fighting for and couldn't articulate it if they had. I saw splinter groups form quickly and easily from within and though the agitators would come from many different backgrounds and many different guises, they all would share one key ingredient; they all wanted to belong.

Humanity would be pared down to the basic model in order to fit the new technology, and when peopled with androgynous, fully compliant chimeras, it would slowly begin to slide back into the swamp. Far into the future, mathematics would again be the universal language, and all currency would be measured in energy. The heat signature from electromagnetism and radio waves would eventually boil away our atmosphere and would render the air unbreathable. Outside your city, oxygen would only be available to those who could afford it, a truly devastating prognosis for a bleak existence.

Thankfully I still had a choice, as I now operated on a higher harmonic of golden vibrational force. I was an angel of flow and creation, two parts deity and one part man, and I decided right then and there, to burn my path of destiny from this race.

I stopped abruptly in the street and with a quick surge of the pulse, I stepped backwards out of Sherlock's body, and at the same time let go of Grace and every glimmer of hope of love and happiness that still flickered feebly within me. I watched them both walk away. I watched them laugh and then stop and turn to each other. I saw Grace reach up and kiss Sherlock like he had always wanted her to. And she could have him for as long as it lasted, I suppose. I knew they would be happy, at least for a few earthly moments. I smiled after them, turned my face up into the rain and took a deep breath. Then I spun on my heel, picked up a flag from the floor and wandered slowly into the crowd; I had a promise to keep.

ABOUT THE AUTHOR

Erstwhile chef of small repute, Salford-born JP plied his trade for more than thirty years in various kitchens in Florence, Barcelona, Los Angeles and Paris. What little skin he had left, he gleefully shed during the pandemic, finally swapping out the pan for the pen and exploding in a flurry of ideas, which culminated in this, his debut novel, a movie of the same name and the much-anticipated feature 1066 The Battle for England. J. P. has two teenage boys and hides out down on the UK's south coast with his fishing rod and what's left of his sense of humor.

 instagram.com/jp.medhurst.7

 facebook.com/jp.medhurst.7

www.ingramcontent.com/pod-product-compliance
Lightning Source LLC
LaVergne TN
LVHW090604110826
845146LV00001B/262

9798886534702